THE WINSTON AFFAIR

By Howard Fast

THE

Winston

Affair

BY HOWARD FAST

CROWN PUBLISHERS, INC.

NEW YORK

All characters and situations in this novel are fictional, and any resemblance to persons living or dead is purely coincidental.

To IRV

THE WINSTON AFFAIR

☆ *Wednesday 9.00 A.M.*

General Kempton had just killed a mosquito. He sat behind his desk, under the slow-moving ceiling fan, and regarded its smeared carcass with philosophical distaste. Then he took a piece of cleansing tissue and transferred the smear to his waste-basket—trying to recall whether it was Alfred or Alexander the Great who had found inspiration in a spider. "Spiders are chums," he said to himself. "Spiders are nice, friendly small animals."

General Kempton was a large, unhurried and, for the most part, good-natured man. He was both sentimental and imaginative, and like most men who combine these qualities, he was aware of them and countered them with self-imposed attitudes of hard discipline. But as his weakness was bolstered by strength, so was his strength riddled with his weakness; and in this he was perhaps not too different from other Theater Commanders.

Sergeant Candyman, who knocked on the door of the general's office and was instructed to enter, was as knowing as anyone concerning some of the general's strengths and weaknesses. He heard the news of the mosquito with solicitude and shame, and thereby punctured the general's annoyance.

"God damn it to hell, Sergeant," the general said, "you have a sinecure here and you use it very badly, if I may say so."

"Yes, sir."

"Misuse it."

"I do my best, sir."

"Any half-wit whines that he does his best, so just can that. If I ever find another mosquito in this office, I'll send you out to Staten Island, which means the lousiest piece of jungle within a thousand miles of here."

"Yes, sir. You'd be right. It won't happen again."

"Now what do you want?"

"There's a Captain Barney Adams outside, and he says that he has an appointment with you this morning. As a matter of fact, he has, but that's for ten o'clock and it's only nine now. And you have an appointment at nine-thirty with Major Wyclif—he's PR with the Queen's Own Riflemen, which is one of their dandy little regiments, and—"

"You just send Captain Adams in, Sergeant, and when the major comes, let him wait until I send for him."

"Yes, sir. I'll do that."

When the sergeant left, the general went to his desk and took from one of the drawers a large Manila envelope. As he turned with it, Captain Adams entered. The general put down the envelope, looked at the captain and grinned with pleasure.

"Barney Adams."

Captain Adams said, "Hello, sir," rather awkwardly, respectfully. He was uncertain of himself, and very ingratiating in his lack of presumptuousness. He had been ten years younger when he last saw the general; and while he had changed considerably, the general was much the same man.

On the other hand, the general evidenced a very real delight in the man that the boy had become. The skinny, long-limbed and awkward eighteen-year-old of West Point had become a good deal of a man: as the general estimated, a hundred and eighty pounds of well-proportioned bone and muscle, tall and erect and good-looking. Although General Kempton was possessed of no more snobbery or caste-consciousness than the next man in his position, he would have admitted to a special pleasure in a solid American lad, and the son of an old friend as well, coming through it as nicely as Barney Adams had. Barney Adams was out of the old blood and the old stock, and both were qualities you didn't mention these days. Everything was too big, the war, the army, the goals—you wallowed in the bigness of it and you looked sour when British colleagues carried on about such things as line and breeding.

Nevertheless, at such a moment as this, you were permitted your own personal satisfaction. The general accepted his own, and he didn't give a damn whether or not the young captain realized his approval. He was approving the son of an old friend who had a sterling record of courage and devotion to duty, a better-than-average number of decorations upon his breast, a purple heart, and a good name. In addition, Barney Adams was red-headed, handsome and well-spoken. The general nodded at Captain Adams, told him to come over where he could look at all of him, and then shook hands heartily. Then he asked him to sit down and offered him a cigar. Captain Adams shook his head, his smile still shy and respectful. They lit cigarettes.

"What do you hear from your father?" the general asked him.

"Well, sir, he writes every week, and his health is good, as far as I know, but—"

"But he's still smarting and growling."

9

"I suppose he is, sir. It's no secret that he would like to be overseas rather than in Washington."

"It certainly is not a secret," the general grinned. "He's the angriest sixty-four years young of any man I know. I had a letter from him—well, I guess three weeks ago, and he was truly pleased to hear that you were to join my staff. You see, I took the liberty of letting him know, Barney, before you yourself were informed. We collaborated in the plot, so to speak, and it's made both of us very happy, believe me."

"I'm very grateful, sir, and proud, too," Captain Adams said.

"Are you? I'm not at all sure that you have any reason to be grateful, Barney. You have seen a great deal of action, and you were seriously wounded. By all the dictates of common sense and the regulations too, you should have been sent stateside and called it a day."

"I suppose so, sir," Adams agreed quietly, "but I wanted to see it through. It means a great deal to me to have a chance to see it through. I'm grateful to you."

The general liked his response. As a matter of fact, their few minutes together had already given General Kempton a warm feeling. Barney Adams the man had all the best qualities of Barney Adams the boy, and something more as well, and like any Theater Commander, General Kempton had a proper sense of what such material was worth. He felt that he had gained a good deal more than the young man in front of him, and he felt an obligation to be straightforward and bluntly truthful.

"We will finish the gratitude aspect of it right now, Captain Adams," he said flatly. "I needed you and asked for you because I needed you. You'll find that this is a very different place from either Italy or North Africa. Given a condition of war, combat is normal and even healthy, to misuse a word. There's been no combat here since the end of the Burma campaign. Neither is there any comfort here. The enlisted men call this area the ass-hole of creation, and the description, while colorful, hits close to the truth. The weather is rotten beyond description, disease is rampant, and the native population is depressed and miserable. There is an absolute minimum of diversion, entertainment and relaxation of any kind. It is a total malaria district, which means a daily intake of atabrine— and explains why we are all somewhat yellow of complexion, that is excepting those of us who are coming down with jaundice and are just as yellow but for another reason. And on top of all that, we have dual theater responsibilities with our British cousins, who for reasons beyond my comprehension have clung to this land for the past century and a half. A shared command is tolerable in a combat area; in a place corroding with indecision and idleness, it is utterly intolerable and calls for the wisdom of a Solomon, which I do not possess. I do my best—which is what we all do, and which is what I expect you to do, sir."

"Yes, sir."

"So we understand one another, Captain Adams, and we waste no more breath on any discussion of gratitude and favors."

"As you say, sir." Adams smiled. "Whatever feelings of gratitude I have will be unvoiced."

"Good. Are your quarters adequate?"

"I think they are magnificent. You know, I am in the Makra Palace, sir. I never roomed in a palace before."

"The Makra Palace," the general observed coldly, "is a damp, unhealthy insect-ridden ruin—before you write home and tell them that you are living like a potentate. It is the least

11

desirable place of any of our staff quarters, but unfortunately the only place we have now with any space available."

"Yes, sir."

"Now mind me, Barney," the general said, rising and beginning to pace the room. "We have a mixed relationship, and when you were younger, you were a good deal like a son to me. But I advise you as a military man, not as a father."

"I understand, sir."

"Stationed here, you must fear and respect two things, if you wish to survive."

"Sir?"

"Mosquitoes and water. Sleep under your netting. And drink only water blessed by the United States Army or well laced with good whisky. Do you understand?"

"Yes, sir."

"Good. That completes your indoctrination." The general stopped pacing and turned to stare at the captain, who rose. "No, sit down, Barney," the general said. "Tell me—what kind of a job do you think you want? Have you been brooding over it? Do you have any preferential dreams?"

"No, sir. I thought I'd best leave that entirely to you. Whatever you have for me—" He was going to say that he would be grateful, but he swallowed it. They met each other's eyes. Then Barney Adams was able to put boyhood and boyhood memories aside. As a man, he saw another man who was General Kempton, and he liked him.

"I'm glad you said that." The general nodded. "I do have something at this moment, Barney. We are holding an important general court-martial next week, and I want you to take the case for the defense."

"Sir?"

"You understand, I am asking. This is not an order, Barney.

If you feel it is beyond your capacity at the moment, you may decline."

"Well, sir—just a moment to think, if I may. It is three years since I looked at a lawbook."

"I would gladly give you more than a moment—a day or a week, if we had it, Barney. However, this court-martial has been twice postponed, and the circumstances are such that it can't be postponed again. It's scheduled for Monday morning, five days from today. I know how short a time that is— and the fact that the man I want you to defend is being tried for murder, makes the time factor worse. It means that you are being projected into an almost impossible situation, that you will have to work day and night in a strange place, and that you will surrender the well-deserved right to orient yourself in your own good time. On the other hand, we are at war, and if this was a combat area, you would ask neither time nor favor. Add to that the record—you ranked first in military law at West Point, you had thorough preparation for the Judge Advocate General's Department, and you graduated from Harvard Law with honors. I'm not going to refer to the choice that took you into the infantry. You did what you thought was right. In the normal course of events, you would have your majority or better. That is apart from all this, although your combat experience is to the point—and the point is that you're a well-trained lawyer, an excellent combination of civilian and military training. Now, will you take the case?"

Barney Adams nodded slowly. "Of course, sir, I will. I can make my attitude plain. I'm prepared to accept any assignment you have for me. Only, I don't understand—"

"You will understand. We will give you every assistance conceivable, Barney. And of course I intend to explain the

13

circumstances." The general stepped over to his desk and took up the Manila envelope he had put there as Captain Adams entered. "Here is my personal file on the case. There is a British major outside whom I must see for a few minutes, and while I'm talking to him, you might glance through this file. Then I'll try to explain just what this whole damn thing amounts to."

Captain Adams nodded. General Kempton took him into the outer office, introduced him to Sergeant Candyman, and then returned to his office with Major Wyclif of the Queen's Own Riflemen.

Wearing shorts and a short-sleeved shirt, his long mustache drooping in the fashion of his regiment, Major Wyclif stood stiffly on a narrow line between stern complaint and necessary politeness. He felt that his life and regiment were in the tradition of both. When asked to be seated, he responded with equal formality, and explained that his mission was neither pleasant nor easy.

"I dislike most," he said, "the impression of whining."

"Then let us agree that there is no such impression, sir," General Kempton assured him. "We have our obligations."

"I don't quite understand that, sir," Major Wyclif said with some asperity.

"The war—the theater. Unity, of course. And to ourselves. What I am trying to say, Major Wyclif—and I don't want to seem sentimental over it—is that we are very close, the same breed and the same language. Perhaps that is why these things happen."

"Then you know what happened last night?"

"I know that there was a fracas in a house of ill repute, and that two of your men were roughed up somewhat—"

14

General Kempton finished lamely and sat waiting behind his desk.

"Roughed up? Is that what you would call it in the States?"

"As I heard it," General Kempton answered softly, controlling himself very well indeed and wondering how abject, properly speaking, a Theater Commander should be before a British major on an occasion like this. He toyed with a mental image of throwing the major out, and the chaos which would follow. He sighed sympathetically.

"One of them has a fractured skull," Major Wyclif said pointedly. "He is in the hospital."

"I had no idea it was as bad as that. Will he be all right?"

"Fortunately, he will. The other lost two teeth and suffered a broken jaw. It's a rotten business, sir—I think you will agree with me."

"I do agree." Kempton shook his head. "A dirty, filthy business. As I understand it, there were two of your men and five of ours. A scrap is understandable, but this kind of business, Major, turns my stomach. Rest assured. The men have been placed under arrest, and they will be tried."

"We appreciate your support in this, really, sir—I can't say how much." The major softened considerably. "But the fact of the matter is not punishment but a general worsening situation. I talk for General Cunningham, you understand, sir, not for myself. He stressed, particularly, this affair of Lieutenant Winston. If that can be cleaned up, then at least on our part we can make efforts at better relations."

"It will be cleaned up—within a week. You can pass that on to General Cunningham, as coming from me."

"Thank you, sir."

General Kempton replied that he did not want to be thanked for what was his plain and simple obligation and duty.

15

☆ *Wednesday 9.45 A.M.*

Sergeant Candyman seated Captain Adams in the waiting room, so to speak, which was space between the outer office—where four sergeants and two lieutenants, first and second respectively, worked at old wooden desks—and the wall which separated the general's office and three other offices, occupied by various colonels and majors, from the long, partitionless front of the building. This space was railed off and about a dozen chairs were lined up against the rail. There were also two low tables which held magazines and ashtrays. On the tables were old copies of *Life*, *The Saturday Evening Post*, *Yank*, *National Geographic*, *Esquire*, *Time*, and *The Infantry Journal*. There were also several copies of *Punch*.

"Now you can just browse among these stateside magazines," Candyman said. "If I say so myself, they are the finest collection in the theater. I put them together myself."

"Thank you, Sergeant. I have something to read."

"Of course. Feel free to do so, Captain. Mine was merely a suggestion. Do you need cigarettes, Captain?"

"I'm well supplied, Sergeant."

"Good. I like to know about such things. Your comfort is my duty and my pleasure, Captain. The Coca-Cola machine is down against that wall over there. Sergeant Miller—the

16

one with the beady eyes over there—he keeps the dimes. It is the courtesy of the house for senior officers who are here on business."

"Why only for senior officers, Sergeant?" Adams asked curiously.

"Junior officers are very thirsty and without a significant sense of dignity or restraint. They would empty the machine three times a day. We can't have that, can we, sir?"

"No, I guess you can't."

"Captain, would it be presumptuous on my part to ask where you were wounded?"

"You mean what part of my body?" Adams smiled.

"No, indeed, sir. I mean the theater."

"It was in Italy," Adams said.

"Oh! Well, we also serve who stay at home and wait. Italy, you said?"

"Italy."

"Thank you." The sergeant nodded and returned to his desk.

Then Barney Adams opened the portfolio and began to sort through the documents, scanning a page here and there. But whenever he began to read, his thoughts would wander. He had come a long way and much had happened to him, and he had a sense of great distances and great loneliness. He strove for the mental discipline that would reassure him and convince him that he did not want to be home.

☆ Wednesday 10.15 A. M.

Captain Adams watched the general and waited. Kempton was one of those large, well-fleshed men whose calm façade and controlled facial muscles simulate repose; but he was always a little weary from the struggle he fought against his own nerves and sensitivities. He had been smoking cigarettes before; now he puffed on a cigar. He had an almost unnoticeable habit of clicking the thumb of his left hand against the pinkie nail of his right hand. A mist of perspiration lingered upon his brow and temples; it had been there before, it was there now.

All of this, Barney Adams noticed. He sat behind his own façade, the good-looking face, the clear, untroubled blue eyes, and the soft red hair. It would have surprised General Kempton to know with what detail Barney Adams noticed and itemized, for no matter how much men—Kempton among them—recognized and honored Adams' courage and excellent manners and good humor, they did not quickly give him credit for being clever. His record was ascribed to an earnest and satisfactory intelligence; he himself did not regard cleverness as a virtue to be paraded, and the knowledge that it troubled those around him added to his own uncertainty. Just as he was never consciously polite, so was his modesty quite unconscious; and out of this combination, those who knew him also knew that he would go to the top. It was accepted that a long and rewarding army career lay before Barney Adams, and General Kempton emphasized this before he went on to anything else.

At the same time, Adams had the advantage, for he knew a great deal about Kempton, about the older man's hopes and dreams and bitter luck and wretched frustrations—whereas the general, accepting Adams so readily, knew nothing of any depth or importance about him except that he was the son of an old and dear friend. It might also be said, in all fairness, that Barney Adams knew very little about himself; and thus he neither disputed nor regretted the assumption of what lay ahead for him. He had never thought about his assignments very differently.

"The point is," said General Kempton, "that I want your steps to be good steps, proper steps. And I think that this is a proper step, Barney. I am breaching neither good taste nor procedure when I tell you that you will have your majority when this court-martial is finished, Barney, and in good time I want to let your father know that I have a full colonel, name of Barney Adams, on my staff. I make no promises; I don't have to. You have three generations of notable military careers in your family. I don't think it could be otherwise."

"That is very kind of you, sir."

"Not at all," the general said. He sat on his desk, puffed his cigar and gestured toward the portfolio. "How much of that have you read?"

"Only a few pages carefully. But I've scanned through all of it. It doesn't appear too complicated as a case."

"The picture is plain but the frame is God damn complicated, Barney. The one takes a few minutes in telling; the other involves a century and a half of history and misunderstanding. Five days from now, you will know the facts far better than I do. But I don't think anything can be altered. There is no confusion of guilt or circumstances—nor is there the slightest doubt about the facts. A Sergeant Arnold Quinn of the British Army was murdered by Second Lieutenant Charles Winston of the United States Army. It happened four weeks ago at a little way-station on the narrow-gauge railroad, a place called Bachree. Sergeant Quinn was unarmed. Lieutenant Winston shot him four times, using his service revolver. There were witnesses to the crime, and the accused man has confessed. All this you must have gathered out of the file—even with a cursory reading."

"Yes, sir. It seems to be one of those sordid and unhappy things that happen when a great many men are armed. Sometimes I'm amazed that it doesn't happen more often."

For some reason, the general appeared to be surprised by Adams' remark; Adams noticed his glance and raised brow.

"I gather it doesn't end with the crime itself?" Adams said.

"It doesn't."

"And I imagine it created bitter feeling among the British."

"Oh, the feeling was already there, Barney. This simply made it murderous. It's no secret that all is not joy and brotherhood with our British cousins in this theater, and it's small consolation, if any, to say that I inherited it when I took command six months ago. I'd like to imagine that things are better since I have been here, but the plain truth is that things are worse. There is literally no day that goes by without some incident between the British troops and our troops, and just between us, the provocation is more often on our part than theirs. I've become so adept at apology that I do it in my sleep. Take this matter of Major Wyclif, who was in here a

20

few minutes ago. Two of his enlisted men got into a scrap with some GIs in a cheap bordel here. The British soldiers were badly beaten and the place was wrecked. Now the NCOs will cover for the men and the junior officers will cover for the NCOs. I am not going to institute a spy system. I make my apology, for what it is worth, but even apologies wear thin. Are you familiar with this kind of thing between ourselves and the British?"

"I've seen something of it in Africa and Italy. But it works itself out in combat, I think."

"Exactly. But in a situation like this, it does not work out. It festers and becomes worse and worse. Myself, I like the British. That's not a politic statement. I like them; I enjoy their company, and there are many things about them that I admire. But mine is a minority position. Too many enlisted men do not like them, and the feeling is returned—and that is no damned good. This theater is like a pivot, the Jap war on one side of us, the European war on the other. We have two large armies in a strange colonial land, and neither is looked upon with any affection by the native population.

"Yes, I worry about my career, Barney, and I don't want this thing to blow up in my face and blow me with it, but more than that, I'm an army man with a job to do and my country at war. We won't win the war here, but we could take a long step toward losing or prolonging it."

When the general lit his cigar now, his hand was too obviously steady, and Barney Adams felt a sudden rush of sympathy for the big man. It saddens most sensitive people to come to maturity and discover that so many of their contemporaries are soaked with doubt and fear; and to have that reaction toward highly-placed men in uniform affected Barney Adams a good deal.

"I hope I can help, sir," he said.

"Of course you can."

"Still, the British know that murders happen. They happen in their forces as well."

"Yes, Barney, they do—but everything was primed for this. The unarmed man, the brutal use of four shots, the revolver, the violence myth—well, it could have exploded everything. The news ran through the British Armed Forces like wildfire, and lost nothing in the telling. I hate to think of what might have happened. I canceled all leaves and imposed a curfew immediately. The British command was as understanding as they could be, but they demanded the right to try Winston in their own court-martial. I couldn't permit that, and finally I convinced them that we must try him ourselves. There is one point of agreement—that for the sake of this theater, the alliance and the war, Winston must be sentenced to death and the sentence must be carried out promptly."

Captain Adams made no response. He sat in difficult and uneasy silence, watching the general and seeking for the proper words to say what should not have to be said.

The general knew, and prodded him, "Well?"

"I wish you had not said that, sir," Adams replied uncomfortably.

"Damn it, Barney, don't you think I appreciate your position? But I had to say it—and a lot of others are going to say the same thing to you."

"Nevertheless," Adams said, slowly and without pleasure, "you cannot ask me to accept a prejudgment of a man I am going to defend. How can I defend him, then, sir?"

"Prejudgment hell! I am talking about the facts, Barney— the trial is up to the Judge Advocate, and I have no intentions

22

of interfering. You yourself admitted that the case is open and shut."

"And—" Adams began, and then swallowed his words.

"Go on."

"No—it's all right."

The general went over to Adams, and squeezed the younger man's shoulder, and said, "Barney, Barney—I busted into this thing like a fool. Say what you were going to say."

"I want to help you, sir. Believe me, I do—and I will, as well as I can."

"I never doubted that. But that isn't what you were going to say before."

"I was going to say, sir—why did you bring me here a week before I was due to report, if the case is open and shut? You certainly have any number of men who can act for Winston's defense."

"Are you asking me fair and square?"

"I am, sir."

"All right. First of all, I want you to have this. I want to give you your majority on it. We don't talk about such things, but I'm laying it on the table. This was a job, and I thought you could do it better than anyone here. Secondly, the facts are open and shut but lousy with inference. Winston is fifty-two years old."

"What? You said he was a second lieutenant, sir."

"So he is—a poor, stupid slob of a second lieutenant and fifty-two years old. Such things happen. This is a large war. Winston was a warehouse boss or manager in Chicago. He has three grown sons who went into the Air Force, so he couldn't live without being in this war. He got the commission through his brother-in-law, who is a congressman—second lieutenant in the Quartermaster Corps. He put on the heat to go overseas, and they sent him here, and since he is evidently not a likable man, they shipped him on to Bachree, which is a stink-hole. When he killed Quinn, a British medico up there kept him from being lynched and sent him to the General Hospital here as a mental case. The psycho officer in the hospital jumped out of his boredom and decided that Winston was insane. First court-martial postponed, and the righteously indignant British chums breathing fire down my neck. Then a wire from Washington—was I taking it on myself to imperil the whole Grand Alliance by harboring a murderer? By what authority or circumstances had I postponed a court-martial? Well, I called a lunacy commission, and they found Winston as sane as you or me—which may not be a great deal but enough to stand trial for murder. I called the second court-martial, and I got a wire from Winston's brother-in-law in Congress. Well, Barney, I am not a hero—maybe adequate with bullets and shells, but that doesn't count. I knew that the army would stand behind a conviction —right down the line—but it had to be a conviction without loopholes. There wasn't a trial counsel in our department here who would put up any better than a sham defense for Winston; there isn't one of them that has the guts to. They are civilian lawyers and they enjoy their commissions and they are not going to buck city hall. There it is. I postponed again and got you here a week early. But I cannot postpone a third time."

"Yet you have decided that Winston must be convicted. What difference—"

"Damn it, Barney, I have decided nothing. I know that the court will convict him, because he is guilty as hell. But I want an honest defense on the record, and to put it bluntly and unpleasantly, I want an army man, a man with a combat

24

record, to conduct that defense. If you feel that I am using you, say it! I am using you."

"We all use people," Captain Adams answered slowly. "I'm not troubled by that—"

"Very well, then. It will do us no good to discuss this any further, Barney. I've placed a jeep and a driver at your disposal and you have an appointment at two o'clock with Colonel Thompson, our Judge Advocate. Between now and the convening of the court-martial, any reasonable request will be granted. If you should want to see me, I am at your disposal."

They shook hands.

"Good luck, Barney," the general said.

☆ Wednesday 11.30 A. M.

The driver of the jeep, Corporal Wayne Baxter, did not suffer from reticence. He was a tall, lean man with sandy hair that needed cutting, and small, deep-set blue eyes. In no time at all, he let Barney Adams know that he was from Nashville, Tennessee, that he was twenty-three years old and had been married for the last five of them, that he had worked at Willie Krause's filling station at the corner of Elm Street, and that he enjoyed the war.

"What do you enjoy about it, Corporal?" Adams asked him.

"Being twelve thousand miles away from the tomato I married, for one thing," Corporal Baxter said, "because anyway that saves me from a murder rap for what I'd do to that bitch for shacking up with any wayfarer comes whistling down the street."

"Oh?"

"I live good, Captain, I eat good. I don't worry."

"Good or bad, I haven't eaten at all today. Where do I find some lunch, Corporal?"

"Well, you got plenty of choice." They were driving down a broad avenue. Streetcar tracks divided the road, and both sides of the road were lined with single-story stucco houses, old and unrepaired, the stucco cracked and flaking away. Skinny brown children played listlessly in the mud in front of these houses. White cattle wandered as listlessly about the avenue, stopping to munch at the clumps of stringy grass that grew on either side of the streetcar tracks. At the street intersections beggars squatted, their begging bowls gripped by their bony knees, their rags drawn over them, as if some chill reached them even in this intense heat. Bearers, their burdens balanced on their heads, stumbled along the broken sidewalks, and rickshaw boys trotted along pulling British soldiers, American soldiers, fat merchants, bald-pated priests, well-dressed ladies, self-important bureaucrats, clerks, civil servants, and any others who could afford the price of a rickshaw. Old taxicabs, driven by turbaned Sikhs, chugged back and forth, and from the distance, like a five-inch shell in passage, came the whining scream of a streetcar.

Every now and then, in the space between the car tracks, a body was sprawled. At first, Adams had thought that these were sleeping people; he realized presently that they were dead.

26

"If you want to eat outside the army," Baxter went on, "there are the Chinese restaurants, maybe a half a dozen good ones, and you don't need to worry about the runs there. There are some others too, the Hotel Grande and the Hotel Britannia and the limey Senior Officer's Club and the Yellow Sea Bar. If you stick to regular issue, you got your Senior Officer's Mess at the big barracks on Kitchener Boulevard. They also cook a nice spread at the Makra Palace, just for the population of the place, but then you got to sign for lunch or dinner in the morning, because they only buy enough chow each day for what they got to feed."

"We'll make it the Senior Officer's Mess," Adams said, and then as they turned off the street, he asked Corporal Baxter about the bodies between the streetcar tracks.

"Dead waugs," replied Corporal Baxter.

"What?"

"I forgot that you come from where the war is, Captain. A waug is a nigger, local variety."

Baxter glanced at Adams and saw his mouth tighten. He shrugged, and they rode on in silence for a while until Adams, unable to restrain his curiosity, asked, "What do they die from?"

"The way these waugs are, skin and bones and rotten with malaria and dysentery and God knows what else, you got to ask what do they live from. Now they say that there is a famine out in the hills, and the waugs come into town and die here."

"You mean bodies are there every morning?"

"There, other places, all over the city. They find a place to sleep and they don't get up in the morning."

"Aren't the bodies taken away?"

"By and by. They start loading the trucks at one end of the

27

city, Captain, but it's like everything else. The limeys don't do nothing like we would do it. The limeys don't do nothing so that it makes sense. I seen the stiffs lay around two-three days in this heat before they got to them."

☆ *Wednesday 2.00 P.M.*

The Judge Advocate, Colonel Herbert Thompson, was a round-eyed, round-faced, bald little man in his middle fifties. He was pink-cheeked, neat, prim, and the shining surface of his mahogany desk was as virgin and nakedly aggressive as if the desk still stood in the furniture shop that had sold it. On the desk was a silver inkstand of native manufacture and two American desk fountain pens. Nothing else. It was as if Colonel Thompson was simply passing through.

Not for a moment was he unconscious of the desk, and he had hardly more than passed the amenities with Barney Adams when he made reference to it, specifying that he did not live or think haphazardly. What should be done, should be done; if it is there to do, do it, and didn't Captain Adams agree with him?

"I admire the attitude," Captain Adams said.

"Thank you, sir. May I say that you come highly recommended. May I say that the honors on your breast recommend you beyond words, sir."

28

"Thank you. You're very kind," Adams mumbled, ill at ease and wondering just what attitude he should take to disguise his distaste for the Judge Advocate. But understanding that, above all, he must cultivate no ill will here.

"I hope we will see a good deal of each other, Captain Adams. I hope your tour of duty in our department will not be limited to the Winston Case. In fact, as I perused your record, I was sorely tempted to defy General Kempton and demand you as a permanent member of my own staff."

"You may feel differently, sir, after I finish this case."

"Well, now, let me tell you something, Captain Adams," the Judge Advocate insisted, leaning forward against his shining desk and poking a pudgy, manicured finger at Adams. "I would feel a damn sight easier if you were prosecuting—I can tell you that."

"I understand that it makes no difference who is prosecuting and who is defending."

"In terms of a conviction—you are right. The man is guilty as hell, and I may tell you, Captain—speaking man to man, of course—that there isn't a senior officer in this whole bloody damned theater who would vote to acquit." When he used words like *bloody* and *damned*, he sucked and tasted them. They were not his words but words for the occasion, and his listener would understand and appreciate.

"Not that I don't have a good trial officer—the best! As fine a man as you would want to shake hands with, Major Freddie Smith, who was eleven years with Willisten, Goode and Cunningham. You know the firm, Captain?"

Adams explained that he didn't know the firm. "I never practiced civilian law, Colonel, or military law, for that matter. But my training at West Point was in military law—that is, what legal training I had there. Afterwards, at Harvard, I

29

specialized in military law. At best, I'm an amateur with a little study behind me."

"Of course it's none of my business, Captain, but I'd be curious to know why you chose the infantry."

His tone was understanding, regretful, with just a shade of condescension, and he tolerantly accepted the slight shrug of Barney Adams' shoulders. "The way the chips fall—eh? Well, I was saying that Freddie Smith is as good a trial officer as you'll find anywhere, but he doesn't have those ribbons you're wearing, Barney. Mind if I call you Barney?"

"Not at all," Captain Adams said.

"We don't have much protocol here, or much West Point either. Not that I don't respect the Point. Turns out man-flesh, if you understand me—good, red-blooded men. And there *is* a war on—we forget that sometimes. Today, Willisten, Goode and Cunningham don't amount to a row of beans; a purple heart and a silver star do."

Barney Adams concentrated on his own face; the flesh became still, the lips set and drawn. He felt suddenly fatigued, tired, empty and homesick, but his face did not change appreciably. He knew his own face very well, the face he shaved each morning and washed each night, the regular and unimpressive features, the childlike blue eyes, the pink lips. He lived with a face that unimaginative and highly paid illustrators for the best national agencies paint over and over—a small boy's face on a man's body, a cheerful, untroubled, unemotional, insensate and vacuous countenance that had become a sort of national pride, that proclaimed the silly, immature, surface jubilance of a people who had never dared seriously to confront themselves aloud. Nor did he pretend that he had ever confronted himself; but he knew his own face; he relied upon it, as he knew, more than was good for himself or for

30

any man; and he faced Colonel Thompson with it, only permitting himself to think: Now he will ask me to call him Herb. Call me Herb, Barney. We're not at the Point, are we?

Adams was wrong. Colonel Thompson spoke one word, forthrightly, "Right?"

Adams nodded.

"Of course—and I wanted you for the trial officer. I told General Kempton that it was our business"—punctuating his words by stabbing his forefinger at the shiny desk-top—"to make the prosecution airtight, solid, beyond question solid. Let the whole world look at it, and they would say: There, by God, is due process! Well, sir, he saw it differently. He runs the theater, not me, praise God. He wanted a solid defense, and he's got it, if I know my man. Just as well. There's too much talk that Winston will hang as high as Haman because our British cousins want it. Sure they want it, and they've got every right to want it. Sure it's important, and the unity of this theater is important!"

He rose, leaning across the desk toward Barney Adams. "But more important is the fact that this man is a murderer! And he will die because murder cannot be tolerated!"

The judgment hung in the air. Adams drew a deep breath and remained silent.

"Well, sir?" the little man demanded, sinking back in his chair and wiping the sweat from his shining pink face.

"I am his defense counsel," Adams said softly.

"Of course—of course. The general spoke of you so much that I keep forgetting you only arrived last night. I accept you as one of the family. Tell me, Captain Adams, are you familiar with the case?"

Adams nodded at the Manila envelope on his lap. "I read

through the general's file during lunch. To that extent I'm familiar with it."

"How do you see it?"

"Well, Colonel, as I said, I've read through the file."

"The essence is there. I've sent the general duplicates of every pertinent document. It's not a complicated case."

"May I smoke, sir?"

The colonel took an ashtray from a drawer in his desk and watched Adams light a cigarette.

"I take it you are familiar with the procedure of a general court-martial?"

"In the academic sense, yes, sir, I am."

"But you've never actually seen one function?" Thompson asked him.

"Not a general court-martial, no, sir."

"Then it behooves us to put on a proper show, doesn't it, Barney? And we will. For your part, sir, you can call all the witnesses you find necessary to establish due process. It should be a memorable occasion—something to add to your many and varied experiences."

"Yes, sir, I am sure it will be." Barney Adams nodded. "But if I might ask you a question or two, sir—concerning the case?"

"Two or twenty. Fire away, young man!" Thompson was the benign executive now. He had stamped Barney Adams with his approval and had embraced him into the "family."

"As I understand it, Winston was brought down from Bachree and admitted to the psychiatric section of the General Hospital here."

"Correct."

"Then there was some presumption of insanity?"

"There was *presumption*, sir. He never should have been

32

admitted, Barney—between you and me. And I'm not alone in that opinion. Not by any means."

"I won't argue that, sir. But once the medical officer signed him in, this medical officer or whoever was in charge of the psychiatric section would have to write a report on his case and present the report to the commanding officer of the hospital. Or am I wrong, sir?"

"Oh?" Thompson remained neutral and noncommittal.

"I spent five weeks in a general hospital," Adams explained.

"You happen to be right, Captain. I believe that is a recognized procedure."

"I can't find either the report or a copy of it in this file."

"For obvious reasons, Captain. The Judge Advocate never requested the report."

"What?" In spite of himself, it came out—burst out.

"You seem surprised. I don't find that so strange, Captain. The defendant was discharged from the hospital—in good health."

"But who discharged him, sir?"

"Colonel Burton. The commanding officer at the hospital," Thompson answered, smiling helpfully as if he appreciated and understood Adams' interest but desired to underline the fact that such interest was no less academic than the case itself. "I'm sure that his report is in your file."

"Yes. But if I may say so, sir, it is not a medical report. It is simply a statement that Winston, having been pronounced sane and responsible by the lunacy board—of which he himself was chief member—was then discharged under armed guard to the Provost Marshal. By the way, sir, where is Lieutenant Winston now?"

"In the Central Guardhouse, Captain. I've given orders that you may see him whenever you desire. And if I may make a suggestion, I would see him today, if I were you. There is your best source of working material—the man you must defend."

"Yes, sir."

"Not that I don't approve of a thorough knowledge of the facts as a basis for a case, but we are simply attempting to set up a sturdy display of due process. Even Winston himself presses for a conviction."

"Sir?"

"Yes, indeed, Captain. I am not coloring my words. He has confessed freely, and now he desires only to have the sentence passed and to get it over with."

"Nevertheless," Adams said, slowly, quietly, but with a persistence that Colonel Thompson was beginning to find tiresome, "I have been ordered to undertake his defense, and I think that I must do so."

"Check! Right to the point, sir! And what else have we been trying to do, but to help you in every way possible, to expedite matters. Remember, Barney—we have lived with this case for weeks. We have wept and bled over it. And now there is nothing we want more than to finish with it and wipe the slate clean. That is why I say to you—go to the jail. See Winston. Talk to him. Get his point of view. And then relax for a week end before the trial. Our British colleagues have a very passable club here, nothing like the grass at home, of course, but very decent. You do play golf?"

"A little," Adams nodded.

"There you are. Now, would you like me to call the Provost and have them roll out the red carpet for you?"

"I don't think so, sir."

"Oh?"

"I would like to talk to Colonel Burton. If you have no objections, sir?"

Suddenly the fat little pink-cheeked man showed an edge, not much of an edge, but nevertheless an edge, sharp and keen. "You know that I have no objections, Captain," he answered. "You have the right to speak with or call any witness you please. Certainly you learned that at West Point, Captain."

"Yes, sir, I did."

"Then you have every right to talk to Colonel Burton. It may be that my own knowledge of military law is cursory, but I would suppose that your first duty would be to your client."

"I agree with you, sir—after the fact."

"What fact?"

"The fact of myself, sir, the uniform I wear, the..." Adams paused. The Judge Advocate was annoyed now, and that was not what he had ever intended. He finished lamely, saying, "I am sorry, sir. I don't think I make myself plain. It's a good many years since I have opened a lawbook, and this is not as easy for me as for those of you who keep a hand in it always."

"Of course," Colonel Thompson agreed with a smile. "The idea is to get a foot wet. Then just plunge in and swim."

☆ Wednesday 4.30 P.M.

Four white cows barred the path of their jeep, and stood there, looking at them stupidly. Traffic piled up behind the jeep. Corporal Baxter leaned on his horn, and behind them the Sikh drivers joined in the chorus until the whole street screamed and wailed with sound. A small, thin man in native dress observed the situation thoughtfully, and then without any great show of force or persuasion, he led the cows out of the way.

"Mother-loving waugs talk the cows' language," said Baxter. It annoyed him that the captain limited small talk. Baxter liked talkative people.

They drove on and came to a square block given over to an open pool of dirty water. Brown-skinned boys, clad only in loincloths, were diving and swimming and shouting gleefully. It occurred to Barney Adams with something of a shock that this was the first laughter he had heard today.

"If the water was clean—a swim would be good in this weather."

"That's no public pool," said Baxter. "It's a ghat, a ritual bath. It fills up in the rainy season, and that water festers and stinks all year through."

Adams shook his head.

"What the hell—there are plenty of waugs. Reproduction, that's the big industry here."

They drove on, twisting and turning until they reached a wide boulevard that ran on toward the edge of the city. This avenue was lined with houses that seemed originally to have been built after the style of the great palaces in the center of the city, but smaller, their domes no more than ten feet across, their minarets reminding Adams of the decorations on roadside drive-ins in California. Then, beyond the houses, for about half a mile the boulevard was lined with clay huts, windowless, formless; and women and children crouched at the doors to these huts, their apathy full of hunger and the fatigue of sickness.

Then there were fields, with here and there a flat-topped stucco house, and then the long, sprawling bulk of the General Hospital.

Many years before this time, the British had built the core of the hospital as an army barracks. This part was one story high, foot-thick clay walls finished with stucco and painted pink. Around each building, there was a veranda approached through archways; grass mats hung in these archways and, sprinkled all day by water-bearers, provided a primitive sort of cooling system. The U.S. Army had joined these buildings with plywood corridors, and had added a dozen more buildings at each end of the installation, using pre-fabricated Quonset huts. As it stood now, the General Hospital was a full half-mile long, and around it were palm trees and acacias, concealing some of its ugliness.

"Drive around it," said Adams.

"Sir?"

"I said drive around it."

"It's none of my business—"

"No, it isn't, Baxter. But if you're curious, I want to look at it."

"At the hospital, Captain?"

"That's right—at the hospital."

Baxter drove the jeep around the hospital twice, muttering to himself, while Barney Adams studied it searchingly and thoughtfully.

☆ Wednesday 5.00 P.M.

People who meet in odd places for the first time wear masks. They are reborn when they shake hands, for each is new to the other, without history, mistakes or the heavy burdens of shared memories. In this case, however, Colonel Archer Burton, commanding officer of the General Hospital, had the advantage; he knew that Barney Adams was an infantry officer, new to the theater, and assigned by General Kempton to the Winston defense. He also knew that General Kempton had a good opinion of Adams, and that there was some kind of old family or army hierarchy relationship. And he knew that Adams had a service record that made him an asset to the speedy and proper conclusion of the case.

On the other hand, about Burton, Barney Adams knew nothing at all—and could just sense that faint tinge of irritation which marks an ambitious ex-civilian confronted by a Regular Army man.

In this, Adams was right. Burton was an older man, tall, commanding in appearance, and very conscious of himself. Even in this mercilessly hot and damp weather, his uniform was creaseless and spotless, and never for a moment was he unaware of his uniform. He touched buttons, felt his eagles, checked his belt with his fingertips, and constantly shot glances at sleeve and trouser leg. What deep and satisfying feeling his present command gave him, Barney Adams did not know—nor could he know why.

Yet in the huge, sprawling organism of the United States Army, Colonel Burton's story was not singular. He had enlisted in the army in 1940, an end-of-the-road action of defeat and despair. Before that, he had been a company physician for one of the smaller auto firms in Detroit. He accepted a tactful suggestion that he resign, after diagnosing a heart attack as acute indigestion and costing the company more money than they felt he was worth. Before that, he had eked out a poor living with a dwindling practice in Cleveland.

His career had been dogged by a combination of small talent and bad luck, and indeed even his error at the auto plant was a curious case which a much better physician might have misnamed. The fact that his Cleveland practice never netted more than three thousand dollars a year turned his ambitious wife into a carping, pushing shrew, and it was she who had pressed him to accept the offer in Detroit; inversely, his growing dislike for her persuaded him to respond to the mushrooming army's plea for physicians. His commission and his uniform gave him his first sense of worthiness or importance, and he soon discovered that while he was only a mediocre doctor, he did have a gift for command. The fortunate choice of several subordinates with organizing ability enabled him to rise to a position of importance and power.

39

Such, briefly, was his background; but unknown to Barney Adams, who, like so many infantrymen, had an overwhelming esteem for the caduceus on the colonel's lapel. So Adams was almost apologetic as he explained his difficulties at being flung into this case abruptly, and his subsequent bewilderment at finding no copy of the attending physician's medical report.

The colonel, cordial and smiling, had given Adams a chair, a cigarette and a glass of ice water. He himself stood at the other side of his office, calm and knowledgeable.

"That is wholly understandable, Captain," Colonel Burton said. "Your bewilderment matched my own."

"Sir?"

"I simply say that I was equally bewildered."

"But surely you read the report?"

"That was the occasion of my bewilderment." Colonel Burton smiled.

"Sir?"

"Well, I put it to you, Captain Adams. A general hospital is a vast and complex administrative task. This hospital is almost half a mile in length and we have six separate departments, or wards as we call them. Just to walk through this hospital on the most cursory consultive basis is half a day's work. We have two laboratories, four operating rooms. Hundreds of people do their work here, and their work must be supervised. This is not the States, Captain Adams. We have three wards of tropical diseases, malaria, cholera, plague, an assortment of dysenteries, jaundice, eczemas never encountered or dreamt of at home, ringworms, fungoids—in addition to the regular statistical ailments that every theater deals with. In addition, we serve as base general hospital for the Burma war—wounds, infections, invalidism and battle fatigue. That's

40

a very quick survey—a good deal left out. Could you conceive of me dealing with this personally?"

"It's a big and complex job," Adams admitted. "No commanding officer is expected to deal with his command in personal terms."

"Precisely. Well, sir, this report you speak of was the responsibility of the commanding officer in the NP Ward."

"NP Ward?"

"Neuro-Psychopathic. Shell shock and battle fatigue are considered old hat by the new disciples of Sigmund Freud." There was an underplayed edge of contempt in his voice as he said this. "They would like a new science of medicine and a new language to go along with it."

"Then you don't consider psychiatry a science?" Adams asked, his question unassertive and polite.

"Well, sir—I am not throwing psychiatry out of the window. Not for a moment. When you come right down to it, any general practitioner who is worth his salt practices psychiatry every day. So do you. So do I. But the science of medicine remains the science of medicine. When a machine is broken, you put it together. When a man is sick, you operate or you prescribe medicine. Germs are dirty, nasty little buggers, and you campaign against them the way you infantrymen go out against the enemy. We live in a real world, Captain. I don't like people who invent other worlds."

"But to get back to that report, Colonel," Adams reminded him.

"Yes—yes indeed. As I said, the report was the responsibility of the CO—a Major Kaufman. It was Major Kaufman who admitted him to the NP Ward in the first place—and without consulting me, Captain. No, sir. First thing I knew of it, Winston was in there."

"Was he out of line, sir? I mean—is it a matter of hospital organization for you to be consulted on the admission of every patient?"

The colonel looked at Adams keenly, as if he had not actually seen him until now. Adams' face was placid. He lit another cigarette, offering one to the colonel, who refused.

"No," Colonel Burton replied slowly, "I am not consulted on the admission of every patient. I think that is obvious, Captain. But neither is every patient a brutal murderer."

"You feel that in this case Major Kaufman should have consulted you?"

"I feel that Major Kaufman does a good many things that would warrant consultation."

"And did the major write a report on the case?"

"He did, Captain. He certainly did."

"I'm sure you know, Colonel, that in the preparation of any major case for a general court-martial, medical reports that bear upon it are forwarded to the Judge Advocate."

"I am aware of that procedure."

"Then why wasn't Major Kaufman's report available?"

"Because I did not accept it! Because it consisted of mumbo jumbo dressed up in fancy language—and was not, in my estimation, an adequate or intelligent or scientific medical report."

"I see."

"I wonder if you do, Captain. Modern warfare is a little more than pulling a trigger or dropping a bomb. The Medical Corps is a necessary and honored part of the service."

"I couldn't agree with you more heartily," Adams said quietly. "I'm not quarreling with your actions, sir. I have neither the knowledge nor the right to do so."

42

"Well sir, I suppose I'm touchy on this Winston business. No one likes to have a mess in his back yard."

"May I ask, Colonel—did you request Major Kaufman to prepare another medical report?"

"I did."

"And was a second report prepared?"

"It was not. Major Kaufman refused."

"He refused? On what basis?"

"On the basis that his original report was competent and correct in all of its diagnostic details."

"And did you take disciplinary action?"

"Not as such. You see, Captain, as CO in his ward, he has the right to stand by a diagnosis—as according to his knowledge. But I reported his action to Theater Headquarters. He has been on the list for promotion. I recommended that his rank be withheld. I also recommended that he be removed to another hospital as soon as a replacement could be found."

"That seems severe, under the circumstances."

"Does it? Discipline is as necessary here as in your own infantry company, Captain. I could not run this hospital for a day without discipline. And I damn well could not run the Jews in it without discipline."

"I'm afraid I don't follow you, sir," Adams said evenly.

"No—then perhaps you don't have these problems in the infantry. Come to think of it, you wouldn't. I have nine of them in my hospital—including every doctor in the NP Ward. Has it ever occurred to you to wonder how they all manage the medical degrees and the safe berths?"

"I wouldn't know, sir. I had six Jews in my company, but four of them were killed in action and the other two were shot up and sent back stateside—and do you know, I never thought to ask."

43

The silence that followed was long, strained and heavy. Colonel Burton stared at the round, boyish face, the blue eyes and the soft red hair, and found nothing there to read, comprehend or resist. The captain sat in his chair, finished his cigarette and put it out.

"What are you after, Adams?" the colonel finally said.

"I am not *after* anything, sir—believe me. I was instructed to defend the life of a man I have never seen and about whom I knew nothing."

"A murderer."

"Yes. I did not choose his crime, sir. Neither did I choose the job of defending him—which I do not relish. Nevertheless, it's my job now. I would like a copy of Major Kaufman's report."

"Am I permitted to ask your purpose, Captain? Winston was examined by a lunacy commission. He was found sane. What are you trying to rake up?"

"You were the head of that commission, Colonel Burton?"

"Entirely proper!"

"I didn't say it was improper. I am not arguing anything. I only want a copy of the medical report."

"I don't have a copy."

"Then I shall have to go to Major Kaufman."

"Must I remind you that I am commanding officer of this hospital, Captain?"

"With all due respect, sir," Adams replied, "may I remind you that I am defense counsel in a general court-martial? I have access to any pertinent material I desire—and to any officer or enlisted man in the United States Army, and no one has the right to interfere with my duties or tasks in this case."

Again the silence, long and heavy, until Colonel Burton went to his desk, picked up his telephone and asked for Major

44

Kaufman. He listened for a moment—then replaced the phone and told Adams that Kaufman had just left the hospital.

"Tomorrow is his day off," the colonel said.

"Then I will be in to see him on Friday, Colonel Burton."

Outside, Baxter was dozing in the jeep. "Where now, Captain?" he yawned.

"Where I can get a double Scotch and wash a taste out of my mouth."

☆ Wednesday 9.20 P.M.

At a few minutes past nine, Barney Adams decided to shave, for it would save a little time in the very early morning he had planned. He was standing in his room at the Makra Palace, in front of a washbasin carved out of green alabaster, and looking unhappily at himself in a great baroque mirror, when there was a knock at the door.

"Who is it?"

A careful yet worldly voice told him that it was Sergeant Candyman from Headquarters.

"Come in, Sergeant. The door is open."

The sergeant came into the room, cast a thoughtful glance around the place, and then informed Adams that even though he had a message from the general, no answer was expected tonight, and the captain might as well finish shaving.

"Sit down and make yourself comfortable, Candyman," Adams said. "There are cigarettes on the table."

"Thank you, sir." Candyman chose a high-backed chair of teakwood, cane and purple velvet. "This is quite a place. I couldn't sleep in a room like this myself, Captain—not alone."

"How's that?"

"Well, it's the way you always hoped and dreamed that a first-class cat house would be. I wouldn't be able to close the door behind me without leaving a ten-dollar bill on the table."

"That's one way to look at it."

"On the other hand, you'd think they'd put the comfort station in a separate room, wouldn't you?"

"They have their ways and we have ours."

"I suppose so. It could be damned embarrassing under certain circumstances, but I agree with you. Live and let live, sir." He helped himself to one of the captain's cigarettes, lit it and blew out the smoke thoughtfully.

"Are you satisfied with Baxter, Captain?" he asked.

"He's a good driver and he knows the city."

"Yeah, he can drive. But I had some doubts since this morning."

"Why, Sergeant?" Adams asked curiously.

"Ah! He's a hillbilly hood. He don't know the right time. He could get to bother you."

"He doesn't bother me," Adams said through the towel he was rubbing his face with. He put the towel back on the rack, and took the note Candyman handed him.

Briefly and to the point, it read: "Barney, why in hell haven't you seen Winston today? I suppose you know what you're doing. I don't. Just for the record, I had the Provost fill in. The document is enclosed."

Adams then looked at the enclosure: "I, Charles Allen

Winston, do hereby state and declare that freely, of my own will and without any coercion or pressure, I do accept and approve the appointment of Captain Barney Dade Adams as my defense counsel during the general court-martial which will consider evidence in the accusation of murder placed against me."

This was typewritten on the official stationery of the Provost. After the statement, the name was typewritten again, and then came the signature in tiny half-askew letters. For a reason he was not to understand for some time to come, the short statement had a deep effect on Barney Adams. It depressed him and filled him with melancholy, as he stood there staring at it and reading it over.

"Sir?"

He glanced up at Candyman.

"Do you want to write a reply, Captain?"

Adams shook his head. "No—just tell the general that I'll see Lieutenant Winston some time tomorrow. It won't be before late afternoon, I'm afraid. I'm taking the narrow gauge to Bachree in the morning."

☆ *Thursday 5.30 A. M.*

At half-past five in the morning, with the mantle of night just stirring its edges, the Chaterje Station of the narrow gauge was as awake and tumultuous as if night had never been at all.

47

In the smoky flare of pitch torches, bearers staggered along with their bales and bundles, hurrying as best they could to make the incoming train. The train was in sight, casting its long yellow beam of light up the track, hissing and shrieking and whistling.

On the cowcatcher of the strange little locomotive, a brown man in a loincloth and nothing else was precariously perched; he acted as an auxiliary warning, and in between the hysterical clanging of the locomotive bell, he cupped his hands about his mouth and screamed, "Ai-eeee! Ai-eeee! Heads oop!"

For a small man, he had a wonderfully far-reaching voice, a shrill, high-pitched voice that cut like a knife through a thousand other screams and shouts. A station employee, aided by a dozen white-clad native travelers, was pushing a white cow from the tracks, and the native railroad constables, wielding their four-foot-long sticks, were attempting to clear the tracks of hundreds of native men and women, who appeared to feel that the only way of assuring their passage was to remain on the tracks as the train came in. Other constables were struggling to hold back a crowd of at least a thousand more local inhabitants—the crowd already swaying back and forth in a desperate rhythm of urgency to reach the train.

Directly into this crowd plunged a government mail truck, the mail officer in pith helmet and white shorts leaning from the running board and roaring, "Make way for 'is Majesty's mail! You bloody 'eathens, make way! 'Ere's the mail going through! Look lively there!"

Miraculously, the crowd parted without anyone's being ground under the wheels, and Corporal Baxter, quick to see his advantage, drove his jeep into the wake of the mail truck. The jeep drew up to the station platform just as the train, hissing and clanging, rolled in.

48

Never had Barney Adams seen such a train. The little loco-motive with its tall, skinny stack was dwarfed by two tenders piled high with wood. Behind the tenders, there was a mail car and two first-class carriages that might have come off a back lot in Hollywood. And behind those, the rest of the train—six open passenger cars, like the summer streetcars on the interurban runs that Adams remembered vaguely from when he was a small child. The first two of these cars bore at least a full brigade of Ghurka troops; they sat and lay thick upon the roofs of the cars; they were piled into the seats; they hung shoulder to shoulder from the side posts; and in squatting position, they filled the running boards, braced by the legs of those who hung from the side posts. The next four cars were, if anything, even more concentratedly loaded with na-tive men, women and children; and the moment the train stopped, the entire passenger contingent erupted.

Even as they flooded off the train, Ghurkas and peasants and children and naked hill people, the waiting crowd surged forward, sweeping the constables aside, and the entire station platform became a hopeless, senseless swirling mass of shout-ing, pushing, wailing people.

Adams looked anxiously at Corporal Baxter, but he was undisturbed, lighting a cigarette as he said, "God damn crazy waugs—it's always this way."

Two boys of about eleven years scrambled onto the hood of the jeep.

"Now you get to hell down off there!" Baxter yelled.

Their father located them, threw a series of poorly-aimed blows at them and a stream of recrimination. They leaped into the jeep and out of it. The father, a thin, careworn peasant, tried to apologize, shouting to make himself heard.

"You'll miss the train, Captain," Baxter yelled.

Barney Adams awoke from his dream, slung his musette bag over his shoulder and followed Baxter, who, cursing, shouting and flailing with his arms, beat a path across the platform to the first-class cars. As he got into his compartment, Adams told Baxter, "The train is due back down at four o'clock. Meet me here, Corporal!"

"I'll do that, Captain."

The train whistle screamed and shrilled. The bell clanged.

"Take it easy, Captain—" the note of warmth in Baxter's voice was new. He closed the compartment door as Adams sat down. It was the first time Adams had ever traveled in this type of compartment: a long, upholstered bench the width of the car, a door on either side; approachable only along the running boards. Two men were already in the compartment, both of them British officers, one older man a colonel in plaid and kilt, asleep and snoring softly, and the other a bright-cheeked subaltern of twenty-one or so in shorts and short-sleeved shirt.

Coughing and jolting, the train started. Adams looked out of the window down the train, and now, if such a thing were possible, it was even heavier with humanity than before.

"They don't turn over, do they?" he asked the subaltern.

"Never knew them to, Captain."

"Seems top-heavy."

"I know. Don't know why, but they just never seem to turn over."

The train was now puffing and hissing its way through a wretched suburb of the city. In the mud and wooden huts, tiny flames were being blown to life in cooking pans. The lights winked and flickered in the gray dawn.

"New out here?" the subaltern asked.

"Third day."

"I thought I didn't recognize your patch, Captain. Lieutenant Frank Stephans."

"My name's Adams—Barney Adams."

"Going far?"

"Bachree."

"I don't envy you. It's a pest hole. Its only claim to fame is a tawdry murder that happened there last month. I do hope you're not to be stationed there, Captain."

"I expect to be back by four o'clock today."

"That's a relief. I was prepared to be terribly sorry for you."

They fell silent and stared through the window, and then Barney Adams dozed off. His dream through his light sleep was of going by train to West Point the very first time, and his pity for the boy he was then filled him with a plaintive sadness and awakened him.

The train had stopped at a little station. The country was of rolling hills, terraced with tea gardens. The sun was rising and the air was clean and sweet. Barney Adams found himself smiling with pleasure.

☆ Thursday 9.23 A.M.

Bachree was something else entirely. Swinging and swaying, twisting and turning and clinging to the tracks through some unexplainable principle of balance, the train found its way into a noxious jungle bottom. When it stopped at the station platform which a faded piece of wood designated as Bachree, the rain had begun. It had not occurred to Barney Adams that he might encounter rain, and the heat had been so oppressive the day before that he had not even brought a coat with him.

Nor was this ordinary rain. It was, so far as he could see, a structure of water, serious, implacable and earnest. It poured down with the unchanging force of a mighty waterfall, as if its source were absolutely limitless.

There were only four steps between the compartment and the station shed, but in these four steps he was soaked. Under the shed, it was not dry, merely less wet, not only because the roof leaked and the rain splashed, but because the air itself was sodden. With him in the open-front shed were two British enlisted men and a British sergeant. Naked bearers brought mailbags and bales and barrels from the train. The enlisted men piled them in as dry a spot as they could find, and the sergeant checked off the goods. As he worked, he nodded at Adams and said, "Welcome to our watering place, Captain."

"Does it always rain like this?"

"When it rains, it rains like this. And it rains most of the time."

While he waited for them to finish, Adams attempted to light a cigarette. His matches spluttered and would not light. The train whistled, clanged and chugged away. The sergeant lit Adams' cigarette with a lighter.

"Thank you."

A truck had pulled up to the outside of the shed, and now the enlisted men were loading the bales under its canvas.

"It doesn't go far," the sergeant explained, pointing to the shadowy bulk of a warehouse about a hundred yards away, "but one can't trundle it through this rain. Are you looking for anyone, Captain?"

"Your CO. I'm afraid I don't know his name."

"No CO here, Captain. I'm in command at the station, for the time being. We only have eleven personnel here now. The only commissioned officer is Major Kensington, but he's not attached. He's medical officer for eight stations on the narrow gauge and for the airstrip as well. It just happens that he's here today because Thursday's our day for clinic."

"Where can I find him, Sergeant?"

"He's at the medic shack. Why don't you hop into the back of the lorry, Captain, and I'll drop you there. I'd ask you to ride in the cab, but that means at least ten steps through this rain."

"I'll ride in back." Adams grinned. "Thank you, Sergeant."

In front of a small bungalow, the sergeant stopped and leaned on his horn. Adams made the veranda in three long steps, and faced a short, gray-haired man with an enormous mustache and quizzical blue eyes.

"Major Kensington?"

"You have the advantage of me, sir."

"Barney Adams," he said, trying to dry his face with a handkerchief.

"Welcome to Bachree. I'll bring you a towel, and then we'll go inside." He was back in a moment. Drying his face and hands, Adams followed Kensington into a tiny cubicle that was office and consulting room.

As he sat down, Kensington said, "Don't mind your clothes on the chair. Anything around here that water can harm has already been harmed. Tea or gin, Captain?"

"Tea, if you don't mind. And I'll take a rain check on the gin."

"Good. Rain check. I like that, Adams." Kensington went to the door and shouted to someone to bring tea and buns and jam. Then he offered Adams a cigarette and thoughtfully lit it for him.

"The few comforts of Bachree. There are, unquestionably, more wretched places on earth—for whatever consolation that holds. May I ask what brings you to Bachree, Adams?"

"I've been appointed defense counsel for Charles Winston."

"Oh?"

"Yesterday, as a matter of fact. I have a limited amount of time to prepare my case."

"It's a thankless task you chose for yourself, if I may say so."

"I didn't choose it."

"No—no, of course not. We don't exercise much choice about anything these days. But what can I do for you?"

"I'm not sure. But since you were the officer who sent Winston down to the NP Ward in the General Hospital, I thought I would talk to you. I understand that I'm fortunate to find you here."

"I hope it's worth the trip and the wetting. I don't know what I can tell you that isn't already in the record."

The tea was brought in, thick and dark. Adams had his plain, but Kensington loaded his with condensed milk from an open can, explaining, "I think it's the rain gives me such a sweet tooth. I'll leave half my teeth here for sure. Have a bun." He was already digging into the jam pot.

"About the murder itself," Adams began. "Are there any possible doubts? Is it conceivable that Winston is innocent?"

"No. You can rule that out completely, Adams. Not only

54

were there witnesses, but Winston was found with the gun in his hand. From the moment he was found, he made no attempt to deny the crime."

"You weren't here when it happened?"

"No—not when it happened. I was at Sutta, about twelve miles up the line. They rang me there, and I ran down by jeep. It took me about forty-five minutes because the road is very bad."

"About what happened that night, as much as you know. Would you mind telling me? I know you've gone through this before, but I would appreciate it."

"Don't mind a bit," Kensington said. "I was set for a bleak and ugly day here. Fresh company's an unexpected treat. Take the two men to begin with—Winston, the murderer; Quinn, his victim. I won't say I got to know them; to me, they were not men one would particularly want to know or be intimate with. But I did get to observe them.

"You know—a more unlikely pair of pals would be hard to find. Quinn's background was the Liverpool docks. He was tough and brutal, and he looked the part. Young man in his twenties. Weighed better than fourteen stone. When Sergeant Quinn spoke, the enlisted men around here stepped lively. Not a bright fellow. I don't mean background. I've seen some damned fine minds out of the same background. Not Quinn."

"You say they were friends—he and Winston?"

"Call it that. They were together a great deal, and they seemed to get something out of each other—" He paused to stuff a short black pipe and light it. "Damn it, Captain, I'm no psychiatrist. Not even Harley Street. I'm a general practitioner who left an excellent if trying practice in Soho because I had certain notions about this war. But if you want my opinion for whatever it's worth, their relationship was homosexual."

"Do you mean—" Adams began.

"No, no—not at all. We really have the most primitive notions of what constitutes homosexuality. I don't think there was anything physical about this. I don't believe either of them could have coped with the thought or even understood their motivations. Don't forget that Winston was twice Quinn's age. Tall, skinny, depressed type. Overbearing one moment, cringing the next. Mistrustful, suspicious, and not overly bright."

"You don't paint a pretty picture," Adams said.

"No indeed. Murder is ugly and terrible, Adams. Murderers are not pleasant or attractive people. Winston was not attractive, not at all. For one thing, he drank too much—and drunk, he was even less winning. He managed to have plenty of liquor on hand. It seems you American chaps leave such loose ends alone. And he used the liquor to get Quinn. They drank together a good deal. Heaven knows, I don't blame them for that. Evenings in Bachree are hardly inspiring. Winston was a sallow type—this climate is the very devil for the liver—and I warned him about jaundice. But such types don't worry about physical disability. They exist in a foggy haze of immortality."

"Do you mean that literally, Major?"

"Well—again, I am not the man for a proper diagnosis. I believe Winston is insane. I believe he's paranoid. But that is only what I think—" He lit his pipe, which had gone out.

"Were they drinking the night it happened?"

"Oh, yes. Whoever is CO here at Bachree uses a little office over the goods depot—the warehouse, which is the only reason for any personnel being here at all. They were drinking

56

there for about two hours, and as I managed to piece it together from what little Winston could explain, Quinn was ragging him on his manliness. You know, taunts about impotence and that sort of thing—I can imagine how Quinn enjoyed seeing the poor devil whine and twist. Quinn cast doubts about the parentage of Winston's children, and that would strike home."

"Could you say when they started to drink and when they finished?"

"Only what I heard later—you understand, Adams? I was not here at the time. But it seems they began to drink shortly before ten. At about midnight, Quinn staggered into his barracks. He woke Sergeant Johnson, the man who met you at the station. Johnson shared a cubicle with Quinn, and the two of them were separated from the other men by a semi-partition. The barracks has a door at each end. You can go directly into Quinn's section or into the other section. When Quinn awakened Johnson, Johnson noticed the time. He helped Quinn, who was quite drunk, to get his shoes off. Then they both went to sleep.

"An hour or so later, Johnson was awakened by the sound of a man swearing hysterically."

"Swearing?"

"Cursing. Screaming the curses. That's how Johnson described it. Johnson switched on the light by his bed, and there was Winston standing over Quinn, holding his revolver at Quinn's head, and cursing him. Before Johnson could gather his wits, Winston began to shoot. His first bullet killed Quinn —took him directly in the face. Three other bullets entered his body. Winston emptied his revolver—two bullets went wild. Before he finished shooting, there were men in the doorway to the main part of the barracks. So you see there were sufficient witnesses."

"Did they take Winston then?"

"No, he held the gun on them and backed out into the night. Men waked out of sleep don't count shots. They didn't know the gun was empty. Johnson sent one of the men to telephone me. Then they dressed and went to look for Winston. Just before I arrived, they found him in the goods depot, but they waited outside until I had examined Quinn. Of course, there was nothing I could do for him. I went over to the depot then. All of the men were outside waiting for me—your men and ours. It's to their credit that they worked very well together."

"There was no antagonism?" Adams asked curiously.

"Oh, no. There had been friction. Saints would snap at each other, holed up in a place like this. But this night, they all worked together and took their orders from Sergeant Johnson. They seemed to share a sense of tragedy—tragedy beyond the fact that two wretched men had destroyed each other."

"Did Winston resist?"

"No. No, he didn't. I went into the goods depot alone—not because I'm a brave man. I assure you, I am not. But a physician carries a shaky kind of immunity with him, and I was also quite certain that I was in no danger. I felt that I knew what had happened—and that Winston's play of violence was over. I was right. Winston was sitting on a box. The gun had fallen to the floor. His hands hung by his sides, and his eyes were open and staring blankly at nothing at all."

"Did he recognize you, Major?"

"Not at first. But after I spoke to him several times, he began to answer."

58

"What did he say?"

"At first—only, Hello, Major Kensington."

"Did you ask him what had happened?"

"I tried and kept trying. I got only fragments—the bits about the drinking session."

"Did he know that he had killed Quinn?"

"No. He didn't remember that."

"You're certain?"

"Quite certain." Now the major turned his head and looked out of the window. "Rain's over," he said. "Are you sure you won't have a bit of gin, Adams? A man can't drink alone at this hour of the day, and I want a drink."

"I think I do, too," Adams said.

Kensington took a bottle and two shot glasses out of the desk. They swallowed the gin neat. Outside, the ground steamed in murky yellow sunlight. Kensington looked at Adams thoughtfully.

"It's none of my business, I suppose, but what made you come out here to Bachree?"

"I thought I made that clear."

"Did you?"

"I thought so."

"I don't know. There's nothing here or anywhere else that could change the fact."

"What fact? That Winston is a murderer?"

"No. That he must die," Kensington said.

"He is going to be tried."

"Oh, my eye, Adams. You're no fool, and I'm not the worst judge of men. You are by no means the tintype you make yourself out to be."

"Thank you, Major."

"Now don't go and take all kinds of umbrage over that. I

bore with you very patiently. I'm isolated here, Adams, but not so isolated that I don't know what a *cause célèbre* this Winston business has become. I read a few things, and the jungle is no barrier to gossip. As a matter of fact, I get the *Times*. A bit late, but I get it. Whitehall and Washington have both washed their hands of Winston. He'll be hanged as a symbol of unity."

"And then all will be well, Major?"

"All is never well."

"No, I suppose not. Why are you so certain that Winston is insane? Because he murdered Quinn? Couldn't he have had more good and sane reasons to murder Quinn than you and I would have to shoot down a Jap if he should walk out into that clearing?"

"That's an old philosophical approach, Adams—old and well-worn."

"I am not trying to be original or clever. I am trying to understand something that is very difficult for me to understand."

"Why? You still haven't told me what brings you here."

"Wouldn't it be easier for you to tell me how you know Winston is insane?"

"All right," Kensington agreed. "I'll play the game your way, Captain Adams. I suspected Winston for a paranoiac before the murder happened. Twice he cornered me and talked to me at great length. You see, he knew why he had been sent here."

"He knew?"

"I talk of his own subjectivity. He believed that there was a great international plot, and that he was the nexus of it. He believed that his own talent was such that he should have held a general rank—and that, holding such, he could end the war

60

within weeks through a solution of every logistical problem. He had a theory that logistics was the key to the victory. But the plot woven around him had degraded him to a permanent rank of second lieutenant."

"He believed that? He actually believed it?"

"Why are you so surprised, Adams? We all have our pet areas of unreason. He made it sound quite logical."

"And who did he think was in this plot?"

"According to Winston, a great many were in it in one way or another. But at the center of it—international Jewry, the Elders of Zion, the whole kit and kaboodle of Nazi filth."

"That makes no sense at all," Adams said hopelessly.

"No. Of course not. The man is insane."

"But he couldn't have put it that way. He must have realized that you would not sympathize with his delusions."

"Adams, your paranoiac shapes the outside world to fit his own purpose. He didn't put it to me that way. Of course not. His wheedling and whining was to help him get out of Bachree—so that he could go about winning the war. He let drop this and that, and I put it together."

"And yet you took no action?"

"For heaven's sake, Adams, what action was there to take? I'm a British medic. I can't go interfering with you fellows, and even if I were so minded, how do you go about accusing someone of insanity? Do we live in a world that enshrines sanity? I have my hands full maintaining my own sanity in this place."

"Yes, of course."

"If you are thinking that I could have prevented Quinn's death, you're wrong."

"I wasn't thinking that. You couldn't have prevented it."

"You won't join me in another glass of gin?"

"Thank you, no."

Kensington poured himself a drink. Adams sat and stared through the window. Now that the rain had stopped, the temperature in the room was rising. He wiped his brow and noticed a mist of perspiration on Kensington's face.

"The rain has a cooling effect. When the sun comes out, it feels hotter than it is. The contrast, you know."

Adams nodded.

"Not a very nice picture of your client—"

"No."

"Well, take it with a grain of salt. I just didn't like the man. What are your own impressions?"

"I haven't seen him yet," Adams said.

"Oh?"

"I wanted to know him a little before I met him."

"I see. You take this quite seriously, don't you?"

"As seriously as I would take the life or death of any human being put into my hands."

"But his life or death isn't in your hands at all, Adams. He is going to hang. There is nothing on earth that you can do to stop that or to change it. In this case, the decision has already been made—and by very powerful people, if I may say so. Why can't you accept that and go through the formality of a defense?"

"Would you, sir?"

Kensington hesitated before he answered. "I deserve that. A physician is apt to forget about personal reservations. I'm a good deal older than you, Adams. It's easier for me to indulge a formality."

"That's an evasion."

"How the devil do I know what I would do in your place, Adams? Is this world so well ordered? Look around you at

62

this happy land. It stinks of death! We're at war. Every day thousands of young men die—strong, alert young men, full of hope and love and vitality. Do you want me to weep and wax philosophical over one twisted, distorted and wretched human being? A confessed murderer. A mind warped with hatred and fear. A personality diseased and damaged beyond hope of repair. Do you doubt for a moment that Winston deserves to die?"

"I don't know who deserves to die," Adams answered slowly.

"Now look, Adams," Kensington said, marking his words with his pipe. "I am not a soldier. I am a physician, and for the big brass I have neither love nor admiration. But this war must be won. Even out here in this stinking backwash of jungle, that remains the central focus of my life. I console myself with the wee bit I contribute, and with the thought that this theater is a sort of pivot. In this pivot, my people and your people do not get along well. There is bad feeling. The Winston affair has brought that feeling to a head. If Winston's death can shorten this war even by moments, it becomes the only positive fact of his life."

"How do you know?" Adams asked sadly.

"Know? Know what?"

"That his death would be the only positive fact of his life?"

Kensington stared at him, angrily at first—then uneasily. Then the major rose and stalked over to a window.

"You'll want some lunch before your train," Kensington said. "I suppose you'll want to look about for a bit." He didn't turn around.

"I want something else, sir."

"What else?"

"I want you to testify at the court-martial."

"Why?"

"Because I feel that your testimony is pertinent."

"I don't feel that it is pertinent or of any importance."

"You will have to let me decide that, Major."

"You have Winston's confession. Sergeant Johnson has been called by the prosecution."

"I feel that I require your testimony, sir."

Kensington whirled on him. "Damn you, Adams, what are you trying to do?"

"What I have to do."

Kensington said slowly, "Can't you understand what it would mean for me to repeat the things I said to you? Don't you understand that?"

"I'm sorry, sir."

Kensington walked over to his chair and slumped into it. Outside, a steam whistle blew. "That's sick call," Kensington explained with a sigh. "You'll have to excuse me for the time being."

"I don't want to have to force you to appear, sir."

"I'll come," Kensington said. "When do you want me?"

"Monday morning. Nine o'clock—at the Judge Advocate Building."

☆ *Thursday 4.20 P.M.*

The narrow gauge was only twenty minutes late. When the train pulled into the Chaterje Station and the screaming mob rushed toward it and the constables beat them back with their long sticks, Barney Adams had a strange feeling of confusion and unreality. On the one hand, he felt that he had not been gone at all; and again, that he had been at Bachree a very long time. A sense of newness and strangeness had worn off.

Corporal Baxter was waiting with the jeep. When Barney Adams climbed in, Baxter asked him, did he want to eat now? Adams shook his head. "No, there's time for that, Corporal. Take me to the Provost now. After that, I'll go to my quarters and clean up."

"Do you want me to wait, Captain?"

"I think so."

Adams sat in silence as they drove to the Provost. Baxter made a few attempts to engage him in conversation, and then gave it up. Barney Adams ranged in his own thoughts. The memory of Bachree became more distant, more spacious.

The prison was an old one, an ugly building of yellow stone which the British had turned over to the American Command; but if it was damp inside, its heavy walls also gave it a certain amount of protection from the sun. There was a visiting room of sorts, where Barney Adams waited after he sent his name in. A Captain Freeman came out to take him to the prisoner.

As they walked down a long corridor of barred doorways —which reminded Adams of a medieval dungeon—Freeman explained that most of the cells were empty. "Only the worst cases. We keep the small-time offenders in the divisional guardhouses. We had a kid here who wrote home that he was languishing in a dungeon. It raised a real stink. What the hell, we have worse jails in the States." He was a cheerful man of about thirty. "I hope this won't be long, Captain," he said. "I'm to stay with you, but I got a date tonight."

"It won't be too long."

"You know, I been waiting all afternoon."

"I'm sorry," Adams said. "I'll try not to keep you any longer than I have to. But I want to see Winston alone. Can you wait outside?"

"My instructions are to be in the cell whenever a third party enters."

"I don't think that applies to defense counsel."

Freeman shrugged. They were at the cell now. A military policeman stood on guard duty at the door. "Open up," Freeman said. "This is Captain Adams, defense counsel."

The military policeman took a key from his pocket and opened the cell door. Adams entered with a curious sense of expectancy. Winston was sitting at a wooden table, his head in his hands. There was another chair in the cell, a cot, a tin basin of water on a stand, and a crockery chamber pot. A small bulb burned in a ceiling socket, and there was a small barred window, about seven feet up.

Winston looked up as Adams entered, but on his face there was neither anticipation nor curiosity. He was a skinny man,

66

long-faced and balding. He had pale green eyes, and he wore metal-rimmed glasses. Adams' immediate impression was of a commonplace man, an unimaginative and not overly-intelligent man, but not a man marked by any stamp of brute or criminal. Sitting there in his coverall fatigues, he did not command attention; if the room had been filled with people, he would not have been noticed at all.

"Good evening, Lieutenant Winston," Adams said. "I'm Captain Barney Adams. I've been appointed counsel for your defense."

Winston watched him without interest or awareness.

"Did you hear me, sir?"

Still there was no response from Winston.

His voice hard and insistent, Adams said, "I am speaking to you, sir! You will reply when spoken to!"

Winston blinked his eyes and then clenched them shut. When he opened them, he said, "Leave me alone."

"I don't intend to take up too much of your time, Lieutenant. But I must speak to you. I am counsel for your defense. You understand what you are charged with?"

"Damn it, don't try to make a fool of me!"

"I am only trying to help you as best I can."

"You can't help me."

"I can defend you in court. I must do that, and I propose to do it."

"Why?"

"Because you are entitled to such defense. No matter what you have done, you are entitled to a fair trial and to an earnest and intelligent defense."

"I killed a man, Captain. What defense is there for that?"

"Let me find a way to defend you," Adams said more gently. "I'll find a way. I only want you to help me."

67

"It's too late. I can't help you or anyone."

"No—it's never too late. I can help you, and you can help me by answering my questions—straightforwardly and truthfully. You must begin by trusting me."

A long moment went by while Winston watched him— with fear, with doubt and with suspicion.

"Well?"

"What kind of questions?" Winston whispered.

"Did you kill Sergeant Quinn?"

"I told you I killed him."

"Why did you kill him?"

"Because he had to die."

"What do you mean by that? Why did he have to die?" Winston shook his head tiredly.

"You said he had to die."

"I knew about it then. I don't remember now."

"Are you trying to remember, Lieutenant Winston? I told you that I am trying to help you. Are you trying to help me?"

"Yes, damn you!" Winston cried out.

"Then try to remember."

Winston strained across the table toward Adams, and whispered hoarsely, "Will you believe me?"

"If you tell me the truth."

Winston relaxed for the first time since Adams had entered the cell. Almost matter-of-factly, he said, "When Quinn left, I just waited until I was told. Then I did what I was told."

"What were you told to do?"

"To kill Quinn." He was picking at a pimple on the back of his hand, and examining it intently as he picked at it.

"Who told you to kill Quinn, Winston?"

"God," he replied flatly, still picking at the pimple.

"God told you to?"

"Oh, yes. Yes."

"Where was God when he told you this?"

"Where?" He glanced at Adams, almost in surprise. "In the same place."

"And where is that place?"

"Here," putting his hand on his side. "Right here. He stays here and burns. Not now. After I did it, he went away. It's the same damned thing, all the way down the line."

"You know you are telling me something to make me believe you to be insane," Adams said evenly.

"That's why I don't tell them," Winston nodded, glancing at the door. "I'm not insane."

"Did you tell this to Dr. Kaufman at the hospital?"

Suddenly excited, Winston cried, "I told that lousy Jew bastard too much. He was with them all the time. I should have known. Oh, Jesus Christ, I should have known."

"What, Winston? What should you have known?"

"That he was with them! With them! All the time with them! God damn you to hell, mister, what are you? A lousy kike in disguise?"

Adams stared at Winston in silence now. The anger disappeared. The slight flush faded from Winston's sallow face. There seemed to be almost a physical process of deflation. The eyes saw nothing in particular. They began to blink.

"Is there anything else you wish to tell me, Lieutenant Winston?" Adams asked.

There was no response.

"Lieutenant Winston—"

Still no response. Then Adams saw that Winston was crying. His face did not move or change, but the tears rolled down the flat, sallow cheeks.

Adams turned around and left the cell.

☆ *Friday 9.20 A.M.*

If Barney Adams had met Major Kaufman under other circumstances, it would not have entered his mind to consider whether or not Kaufman looked Jewish. Even with the name, the thought would not have presented itself to Adams. He was simply not concerned with whether or not any man looked Jewish or was Jewish. It did not resolve itself into a matter of principle or tolerance; the problem had been absent in his formative years, and in his maturity he did not approach it as anything that excited either his interest or his curiosity. He had never cared nor had he ever found any reason to care —until the last three days.

Now he studied Kaufman in terms of two men, Lieutenant Winston and Colonel Burton. He deliberately attempted to see Kaufman as a Jew, but his frame of reference was insufficient. He could not make any reliable connection between Kaufman and the Jews in his company, nor could he reliably separate Kaufman from other army doctors he had been in contact with.

Kaufman was of medium height. He was dark, with gray eyes. He had a round face that was badly scarred from a youthful acne, a flat nose, full lips, and a New York City inflection in his speech. He was somewhere in his middle forties.

70

He was neither friendly nor unfriendly, and he was on his guard. He also impressed Barney Adams with the fact that he was a very busy man.

Of the Winston case, he observed briefly, "That's over and done with, so far as I am concerned. It's been taken out of my hands, Captain. I am not interested, and I have no desire to, discuss it." As he spoke, he was glancing through the papers on his desk. He signed two documents and put them into a box labeled *Outgoing*.

Then, pointing his pen at Adams, he said, "There's small virtue in thoroughness, Captain. No one will commend you for it. You tell me that you have to defend Winston. Good. That's your job. I have finished with mine, so far as Winston is concerned. I have over a hundred patients to see today. I don't know what you have to do."

"Very little," Adams replied softly, "and I am afraid nothing of the importance of having to see sick people and help them."

Back at his papers, Kauman looked up sharply. He studied the ribbons Barney Adams wore and asked about his wounds.

"I was very lucky. A grenade exploded behind me, and I got five pieces in my shoulders."

"There's all kinds of luck. Why did you come here?" he asked bluntly.

"That's too long a story to tell now."

"And how do you think I can help you?"

"Well—I suppose the core of it is this. I want to know whether Charles Winston is insane." Then he told Kaufman about the incident in the prison the day before. "I'm asking you because it seems to me that you are in the best position to know. You admitted Winston to your ward. You examined him. You treated him."

Kaufman did not reply at once. He watched Adams thoughtfully for a long moment before he said, "Do you think he was shamming?"

"I don't know. I felt it was too much like a literary notion of how an insane man would act."

"You can put your mind to rest, Captain. Winston is an incurable psychopath. In other words, he's insane. Not only that, but his condition is progressive, with very little hope for even a temporary remission."

"What do you mean by that?"

"I mean that as a personality, Winston is disintegrating. He is very quickly losing touch with all reality. How can I put that to you? His consciousness—his soul, if you will have it that way and admit to a soul in such a man—is turning in upon itself, shortening its lines of defense in a desperate search for survival. But in that search he will be destroyed."

"Physically?"

"No—he won't die. Not yet. Unless he kills himself—which is not unlikely. But as an inhabitant of our world, he will die."

"I'm afraid I don't follow you," Adams said.

"Do you know much about insanity, Captain?"

"Almost nothing."

"That's honest, and if most physicians were equally honest, they would admit to the same thing. The science of the mind is very young, very new, very uncertain of its conclusions. Even our terminology is awkward and unspecific. Winston is suffering from what we classify as dementia paranoides. One might think of this particular case as a formal or almost classical paranoides. Paranoia is a generic term for a whole group of mental disease, but Winston's case is specific and unmistakable."

"And is this organic? Was Winston born with this?" Adams asked.

Kaufman shrugged. "That's something we can't answer with certainty yet. My own opinion is no. My belief is that what we call the 'paranoid personality' comes into being in very early childhood, as a result of the child's environment. Of course, such a thing is not a psychosis—or, insanity, as you might say. It's a neurotic personality pattern which establishes the groundwork for later development. Nor does it by any means always lead to a psychotic state or insanity, with consequent personality disintegration. The paranoid personality is all too common in every walk of life, and the grief and heartache it brings to mankind is almost beyond calculation. But by far the greatest number of such personalities live out their entire lives without ever being committed to an institution."

Adams was intrigued, wholly captivated. "Could you describe such a personality to me?" he asked. "I mean in general terms."

Kaufman smiled and leaned back in his chair. "Only if you accept what I say without argument and accept what you don't understand without explanation."

"I'll try, sir."

"All right. We'll begin with a hypothetical norm. I specify hypothetical because we have no real notion of the normal man as an abstraction. We can only establish a norm out of our own torn and distorted world, and in a general sense we hold that a man who can live in this world, face its realities and cope with them sensibly is a normal human being. That's a loose and amorphous definition, but it's the best we have at the moment. Now, within this situation, a man defends himself against real dangers because he is afraid of real dangers.

73

If he is to survive, he must take care of himself. Do you follow me?"

Adams nodded. "So far—yes. No arguments."

"Now—on the question of the neurotic, a hell of a damn lot has been written. But the simplest approach is to think of the neurotic as a person who compulsively defends himself against unreal dangers—that is, against dangers that do not exist. The mechanism of defense is a natural mechanism; it is the perception of danger that has gone awry. The most frequent, timeworn example is that of the old maid who looks under the bed for a man each night before going to sleep. The old saw is that she hopes to find a man there, but actually she doesn't. She has a great fear of men—one of the reasons why she is a spinster. And since this fear is based on no reality— she would live a more fruitful life with a man than without one—it is part of a neurotic pattern. Her looking under the bed is compulsive. She knows by reason and experience that she won't find a man there, but she cannot resist the force of her unreal fear.

"Of course this is a vulgar simplification of a profound and complex pattern of mental organization."

"But she isn't insane?" Adams asked.

"By no means. She is still in touch with reality. All neurotics are. She knows there is no one under the bed. She recalls experiences. And she is still able to function, in spite of her fears. She simply goes through a compulsive neurotic pattern, and is even able to be somewhat amused at her own nonsensical behavior. But if she should become hysterical upon entering the room, if she should be unable to look under the bed because she knows the man is actually there, and if she sees the man where he is not—well, at that point her ability to deal with the nonexistent danger is collapsing; her neurotic or-

74

ganization of defenses is breaking down, and she is passing into the psychotic state. Of course, this is not a case we are discussing, but a bit of folklore, and therefore it has no clinical validity."

"But even as folklore," Adams said, "are you describing a paranoid personality?"

"Oh, no—far from it. Just from what you have read or heard, Captain, how would you describe a paranoiac?"

"Well—I suppose the way anyone else would, delusions of grandeur, a persecution complex—"

"Yes. That underlines the fact, but it tells us too little. As in all neuroses, your paranoid personality is motivated by fear. He is afraid of people—all people. Somehow or other, the circumstances of his childhood combine to set up a very deep belief that humanity is committed to his destruction."

"Does he know this?"

"Of course that question is basic, isn't it? And the answer is that he does not know it; it is buried too deep in his consciousness. It compels him, directs him, guides him, but for every neurotic action he takes, he must devise some sort of rationalization in terms of reality. Such people are suspicious. They calculate and inhibit every action because they are always afraid of placing themselves in the power of another. They are not capable of love in any full sense; love is dangerous; they fear it. They can make relationships with superiors, out of fear, or with inferiors, out of the security of power, but they can form no deep friendships in the full sense of the word. They are lonely men. For them, war is always. It never ends. And very often, indeed most often, they organize their defense against these neurotic fears of nonexistent dangers in two patterns: total and degrading submissiveness or a compulsive, terrible drive for power. Curiously, these two seemingly

75

opposite patterns of defense are often found in the same person—as, for example, the sergeant who cringes and crawls before his platoon commander but becomes a monster of a tyrant over his own men. You've met that type?"

Adams nodded.

"They mix in the same man. Hitler and Mussolini are the two most notorious paranoiacs of our time—but before he had power, Hitler was a pleader and a whiner."

"Would you call them insane?"

Kaufman thought about this for a moment, then shook his head. "No—not in the sense that Winston is insane. You could say that Hitler and Mussolini are insane in a social sense, not in a clinical sense. In Winston's case, there is a qualitative change that has taken place. From what Winston was able to tell me, there were no memories that did not suggest paranoia. I say suggest, because there was less than a week in which I could examine him. He had an unhappy, lonely childhood. He married a woman who terrified him, a woman he hates and fears, and with whom he has not had intercourse for sixteen years. His three sons apparently treat him with a mixture of contempt and pity. He feared them and envied them, and tried to prove himself and defend himself with this commission. In the warehouse where he worked, he was a petty tyrant—but he lived in day-to-day fear of being fired. After Pearl Harbor, he began to create a daydream, a fantasy of winning the war singlehanded, through his own talent and personality. At first, it was only a fantasy."

"In other words, at this point he was not insane."

"By no means insane. He was a neurotic, an intensely disturbed man with a paranoid personality, but he was not psychotic."

76

"Could you have recognized the possibility of insanity if you had examined him then, Major?"

"I don't know. I would like to think that I could have, but I don't know."

"Was the insanity inevitable?" Adams asked.

"I don't know that either. In Winston's case, I would think so, but I can't be sure."

"Major Kensington, the British medical officer at Bachree, told me that there was no doubt in his mind but that Winston was insane before the murder."

"If I may ask, Captain, where did you see Kensington?"

"I went to Bachree yesterday."

"Oh?"

"Would you agree with Major Kensington?"

"Of course. It is not the act of murder that precipitates the psychotic state. It is the psychotic condition—in Winston's case—that precipitates the murder."

"Would you have any opinion on when Winston actually became insane?"

"Only a guess—and in a case like this, there is no actual moment that you can point to and say, It happened then. The process is gradual, slow at first, and then increasingly rapid to its conclusion. In Winston's case, I would guess that his fantasy of winning the war, or at least being a person of very great importance in the army, absorbed him increasingly. When it ceased to be fantasy—as Winston saw it—I cannot possibly say. At any rate, from what he told me, he schemed, connived, lied and exercised a remarkable amount of shrewdness to get his commission. After that, he began increasingly to think of himself as put upon, plotted against, and deliberately thwarted. He began to erect in his own mind the delusional structure of a vast plot, with himself as the central

77

object. At Bachree, a pattern of latent homosexuality—by no means unusual in paranoiacs—focused on Quinn, who was a homosexual, without any question. But Quinn was not entranced by this skinny, half-mad, middle-aged man, and he used him opportunistically and sadistically. Sooner or later, the numberless amorphous persecutions that Winston believed in had to become symbolized in Quinn. At the same time, Quinn had begun to destroy Winston's defenses. When that happened, Winston killed Quinn. It was cheap, tawdry and brutal. Yet it was inevitable."

There were a few moments of silence now. Kaufman looked at his watch.

Adams was absorbed in his own thoughts; as from a distance, he asked, "Where does the notion of God come into it?"

"God? Oh yes—you told me. As a matter of fact, it frequently appears in the pathological stage. The paranoiac believes that God is in some part of his body, God is with him, literally—a sense of burning, severe pain sometimes. It's a symptom of the rapid personality decay."

"How rapid, Major?"

"In Winston's case? Two or three months perhaps. He is already in deep depression. In the outside world, he would kill himself. In his cell, I doubt it—it would require too much energy and imagination, and I think he is past the stage where he could summon that. His depression will deepen, however; he will lose all will to eat or sleep or see or react. He will retreat into himself, and in not too long a time, he will die. These are speculations, of course—no more." He looked at his watch again. "I'm afraid I must go on my rounds, Captain. If you want to wait here until noon, we can have lunch together."

78

"I'll gladly wait. Do you have something I can read meanwhile—a text of some sort?"

Kaufman took three books out of a case on one side of his office, and opened each to a chapter which he marked with a bit of paper. "I wish I had more here, but I don't. There is a classic essay by Freud, but I don't have it here. These are case histories, and they will help you to understand the process. Two are textbooks. The third is Plutarch's *Lives*, and I think it would interest you to reread his chapter on Alexander the Great. I presume you have read it?"

"In school. That was many years ago."

"Read it again. To my mind, it is the finest literary description of a paranoiac that we have, very clear and very penetrating. It may help you more than the case histories."

He left Adams there with the books.

☆ *Friday 10.50 A.M.*

A rather handsome woman, but one whose face was drawn tight with her own difficulties and tensions, entered Major Kaufman's office and said, "Pardon me, Captain Adams. There is a call for you from Headquarters. I wasn't sure that you were at the hospital, but the nurse on duty thought you hadn't left."

The book open in his lap, Adams looked at her curiously—

aware of how very few American women there were in this entire area, how few he had seen. Was this the first one who had spoken to him, he wondered? He stared at her, and hunger and longing awoke in him. In her nurse's uniform, she was prim and neat and attractive.

"Yes, I'm still here," he replied awkwardly. "I'm waiting for Major Kaufman to return."

"You're from the Judge Advocate, aren't you, Captain?"

He nodded.

"Why can't you leave Major Kaufman alone?" Her controlled anger brought two spots of red to her cheeks. "Hasn't he had enough out of this miserable Winston affair? Why must he be hounded?"

Dumfounded, Barney Adams sought for something to say and found nothing very pointed, except the lame protest that he was not hounding Major Kaufman.

The nurse picked up the telephone on the desk and said, "Give me that call for Captain Adams, Kelly." Then she put the telephone down and stalked out, slamming the door behind her. Adams picked up the phone, and heard General Kempton's voice.

"How are you, Barney?" he demanded cheerfully.

"I don't know, sir."

"You're not letting this get you down, are you?"

"Oh, no," Adams replied. "Not at all. I'm enjoying this, sir. I'm having a fine time."

"That's no way to take it, Barney," the general said comfortingly. "Just walk through it. Now look. The correspondents here have been pushing me. They want to meet you. I can't blame them—the Winston affair is a big story, and they know about you and you make good copy."

"If you don't mind, sir, I'd rather not," Adams said.

"Sure, I know how you feel, Barney. I'd think less of you if you said, Hurray—I want publicity. Every two-bit punk around here wants his name in the papers at home. It's not admirable. But in this case I can't give you an out. I'm afraid you must be there."

Adams held the phone in silence until the general asked, "Barney? Are you still there?"

"Yes, sir. Where will it be?"

"At my office. Three o'clock. Is that all right?"

"Yes, sir."

"Now, Barney—I don't want you to feel that I'm pushing you around, because I am not. Have I interfered with you in any way, tried to direct you, guide you, turn you away from anything?"

"No, sir, you haven't."

"I admit I pressed you to see Winston, but that was only because I want a clear and unimpeachable record. I was a little nervous. Well, you were doing things your way—and I'm leaving you alone. But this press conference is one of the stinking necessities of modern warfare, and I can no more avoid it than yourself."

"I understand, sir."

"I'm glad you do, Barney. I'll see you later."

☆ Friday 12.10 P.M.

"We can offer you hamburger," Major Kaufman said. "They allow a few very old cows to be slaughtered for the hospital menu. But the only way to make them edible is to grind every bit of meat and to kill the taste with whatever spices we have on hand. Sometimes it comes out surprisingly good, sometimes not so good."

"Whatever you have," Adams replied, still lost in the hatred and bloodshed and lust and megalomania of a young Macedonian madman. He had discovered, when he began to read, that he had forgotten Plutarch, as one usually forgets the forced learning of youth; and he was pondering the fact that the narration had left him so unmoved then—only to touch him so deeply and profoundly now at a time when he himself was a part of the most devastating armed conflict in man's memory.

"You don't care much about food, do you?" Kaufman asked.

"When I'm hungry, I suppose. I don't have much appetite in this heat."

"Does it matter to you what you eat?"

Puzzled, Adams shook his head. "Not very much. Is that a neurosis, Major?"

82

"With your face, Adams," the major said, "no one would know whether you were pulling their leg or not—whether you were brilliant or dull, insensitive or sensitive, shrewd or stupid. You could just look at them. You could go through life with that face, Adams, and you could hardly be a failure."

Controlling himself, trying to guess what had happened to Kaufman during the time he had been gone, Adams answered quietly, "My face is not under consideration, Major. Another time, perhaps, it might make for profitable discussion, but we are both of us pressed for time."

"I was honest with you, Captain—honest and forthright. You didn't have to play games."

"What games?" Barney Adams asked, his voice hardening.

"Why didn't you tell me you had been to see Colonel Burton?"

"Because I thought you knew."

"How? I was on leave. I came on duty an hour before you turned up. How would I know?"

"I'm sorry, Major Kaufman. I should have thought of that. I didn't."

"Just as you never thought of telling me that the reason you came to me was to obtain a copy of my medical report on the Winston case?"

"Because I thought you knew that too."

"No—oh, no. It won't do, Captain."

"I'm terribly sorry, sir," Adams said. "Please believe me, it was not my intention to confuse you or deceive you. To tell the truth, once we got to talking I forgot all about the report. That's why I didn't bring it up."

"You mean you don't want it?"

"I'm afraid I do want it," Adams said. "I must have it."

Kaufman took a few paces away, stood for some moments

with his back to Adams, and then turned and observed Adams darkly and unhappily. "You can't have it, Captain."

"Why?"

"Because I have no intention of disobeying the orders of my commanding officer."

Adams closed the book on his knee, placed it on the desk and rose. Watching the major thoughtfully, he lit a cigarette. There were many things he could say, but he wanted to say the right thing, and as it so often happened, he was by no means certain of what the right thing was. He wanted to understand Kaufman, and he knew that it would not be easy. Here was a chasm he had never attempted to cross before. In all of his formative years, there had been a series of neat and correct bridges which were used to communicate with other people, one set of bridges for one kind of person, another set for another kind, a third set for a third kind. It was like taking a recognition course. You learned what was correct for what, and you used it. But for the past two years the bridge system had operated less and less successfully. Now it was no good at all.

"Are you telling me," he asked quietly, almost casually, "that Colonel Burton ordered you not to show me or give me a copy of your report on Winston?"

"Let's say that he advised me not to."

"I see." Adams nodded. "Why don't we sit down and talk about this like two civilized human beings, Major? I never met you before today. You never met me. This morning I behaved foolishly, thoughtlessly—as anyone does who takes for granted a series of premises out of his own head. I think you're taking the wrong attitude now—if I may say so."

"You may," Kaufman replied, "so long as you keep in mind that I can order you out of here, and when I do, you go."

"It's not as easy as all that, Major."

"I think it is."

"Tell me this, Major," Adams said, his voice still soft and even, "have you ever had experience with a general court-martial?"

"I have not."

"I thought not. You see, there is an old saw that an army court is a kangaroo court, a hanging court, a sort of inquisition where a man goes without hope or help. Well, the very nature of military discipline gives rise to that attitude. I suppose it must, for an army trial is trial without jury or superior courts. On the other hand, the army is conscious of this, very conscious, and in an attempt to balance the scales, they have given an extraordinary amount of power and privilege to the defense counsel. There is no document in this theater that I cannot obtain, if it will help me make my case. And there is no officer, including General Kempton, whose presence I cannot demand. You can order me out of here, Major, but I can order you to appear in my presence. And when I ask you questions then, you will answer them because you must. Those are my powers, sir. I have no desire to invoke them. For heaven's sake, let's sit down and talk like sensible people."

"Yes, sensible people," Kaufman repeated. "Oh, let's talk politely and calmly. Let's not raise our voices."

"Yes—I think it helps not to lose our tempers."

"Does it, Captain Adams? How does it feel to go through life being polite and charming and unruffled? You've been in this ass-hole of creation three days, Captain Adams. Do you know what it feels like to be here three months—or three years? Just what do you know, Captain Adams? What are you after? Would you like to give a memorable court per-

85

formance—bring expert witnesses in, make a great name and score for yourself?"

"I have to defend Winston as I see fit."

"Why? Why do you have to defend him? What are you defending? What are you asking me to help you defend? When Burton asked me to rewrite my report on Winston and declare that he was sane, I refused. I didn't have to refuse. I could have scribbled a few words to the effect that Winston was sane and of sound mind. It would have changed nothing. Either way, Winston will be condemned to death. But I refused—because I am a physician, a doctor, not a cheap political opportunist. I refused because I could not change that report and remain a physician—and because I know that some day this war will be over and I will be a doctor again. And I knew the price of refusing—make no mistake about that, Captain Adams. I was listed for promotion; there will be no promotion now. I am a psychiatrist at the head of a general hospital section. A few months from today, I'll be dispensing medicine somewhere out in the jungle. I knew that, and still I refused. And now you ask me to go further—to disobey orders. Tell me why, Captain Adams."

"Because a man is going to be condemned to death—who should not be condemned to death. That is why."

"I see. To save Charles Winston. You want me to help destroy myself to help save Winston. Is that it?"

"If you put it that way—yes, that's it."

"Of course. And it makes sense to you, I suppose. Winston, whose twisted life process revolved around a maniacal hatred of Jews, who is a decaying cesspool of every vile chauvinism and hatred ever invented; Winston, who spat in my face and called me a kike and a sheeny—this Winston, whose soul is warped and corroded beyond repair, whose mind is decaying

86

and dying, who is a self-confessed murderer—this is the man you want me to help you save, even at the price of myself. Yes?"

"Yes."

"I suppose you have thought this through in your own mind, Captain?"

"I've tried. Not entirely. But I seem to have found one thing that I can put my finger on."

"And what is that?" Kaufman asked coldly.

"That Winston is sick—and that his sickness is the world's sickness. Is the answer execution, Major Kaufman? Perhaps it is—and perhaps we are executing the world. Is that what you are trying to tell me?"

Kaufman looked at Adams without answering. Then he walked over to his chair and dropped into it. "Give me one of your cigarettes, Captain," he said.

As Adams lit it for him, Kaufman said, "Let me apologize for what I said about your face, Adams. It was anger, but not altogether pointless. We grow up with the image of that face before us. We learn to love it and to hate it—and to envy it. I suppose I should be mature enough to spill my venom in other directions."

"It's not venom." Adams shrugged.

"Let me decide what it is. We confront each other out of different worlds, Captain."

"I don't think so."

"No? You're a West Point man, Adams—word of your background gets around. You're General Adams' son—and he was staff assistant to Pershing in 1918. They even say that you're part of *the* Adams family—"

"We're not."

"You seem to have done all right without it. Did you ever hear of Rivington Street, Adams?"

"No, sir, I can't say that I have."

"The family seat. The Kaufmans occupied a cold-water flat there. There were six of us—six children. One got killed by a truck. We five fought and clawed and worked our way out of that particular cesspool. I won't bore you with the details of how I got through college and medical school. Sufficient that I did. I became a staff psychiatrist at Bellevue Hospital in New York—then assistant to the chief. I set up in practice. I have a wife whom I love and three children. In 1940, my income was forty-three thousand dollars. I walked out of it because I could not sit on my ass and become rich while others died in a cause that was mine as well. Here I am. When I give you that report, Colonel Archer Burton is going to break my back—and there is not one God damned thing that you or I can do to stop him."

Adams was sitting on the other side of the desk now. He considered what Kaufman said, and then spoke. "I'll leave it up to you, sir. Either give me the report or don't give it to me. If you decide not to give it to me, I will not request it officially."

"You know how I feel."

"Yes, sir—to some extent. But I know that when one tries to put his reasons for some very important action into words, one is very often frustrated. You told me why you refused to change your medical report, and perhaps that was one reason why. But not the main reason. Not the real reason."

Kaufman did not answer immediately, and at this moment an orderly entered with their lunch. Adams did not press his point, and they ate in a curious silence. The hamburgers were small and had been fried in deep fat. They were quite good, but the mashed potatoes and beans that came with them were cold and tasteless. Adams realized that he would hardly have noticed this had not Kaufman made his earlier comment.

Kaufman poured strong tea for each of them and then asked bluntly, apropos of what Adams had said some fifteen minutes before, "What was my real reason, Captain?"

"I'm not sure that I can put it very well either," Adams replied, smiling. He had a disarming and gracious smile which even Kaufman found hard to dismiss. "But I think it was Winston more than yourself that motivated you. If you had changed that report, all hope for Winston would then be gone. In effect, you would have consigned Winston to death. I don't think you were able to do that, Major Kaufman."

"Adams," Kaufman said slowly, "aside from my medical duties, there was no reason for me to lift a finger to help Winston. I'm a Jew."

"You say that as if it should carry some special and hidden meaning for me, Kaufman. It doesn't. I am a Protestant, but that doesn't make me insensitive or indifferent to what Nazism and Fascism have done to this world. The only Jew I suppose I knew in my childhood was a Colonel Cramer. He was a friend of my father's and a dinner guest on many occasions that I remember. I never knew that he was a Jew, until one evening at dinner he brought up a quotation we had need for. It stayed with me—'Ye are the salt of the earth: but if the salt have lost his savour, wherewith shall it be salted?' After dinner my father expressed some surprise that Colonel Cramer had come up with the quotation so readily. 'Why?' I asked. 'Because he knows his Testament?' 'Because he is Jewish and because the lines are from Matthew,' my father told me. He left it at that. You see, Major, I don't believe in these different worlds that we inhabit, and if I had any such beliefs, they were beaten out of me in Africa and in Italy. I've been in this land only three days, as you mentioned, but I don't feel its strangeness any longer."

"You haven't convinced me that I want to save Winston," Kaufman said.

"I don't have to convince you, because as you made plain to me, Winston cannot be saved. I think you want to save something else even more important than Winston, and I think you know what I mean, Major Kaufman."

"I know what you mean," Kaufman said dully and hopelessly. "I'm no hero. I can't be a hero."

"Unless," Adams pointed out with deliberate cruelty, "the world you value is well aware that you are a hero. But if your wife and your friends and all the people whose opinion you value here and at home don't see you as a hero at all, but just consider you a damned fool—well, then yes; why be a hero?"

"That's a lousy thing to say."

"Yes."

"What skin off your back is it if I live with myself?"

"Nobody lives with himself alone, Major. Whatever it was back there in Rivington Street that made you the man you are today, it wasn't the dirt and poverty. There were other things that you have to remember and live with."

"Do you really think you can win this case?" Kaufman demanded. "Don't you know that Winston must die? Don't you realize that nothing you can do will alter the verdict? How can you sit there and talk as if any action of mine would make a difference?"

"Because it would make a difference."

"Adams—tell me, isn't unity and harmony in this theater of action more important than the life of a pathological murderer?"

90

"You don't buy unity with a man's life or with injustice or with a fixed verdict."

"How can you be so damned sure of yourself?"

"Because I'm unsure of myself. It's not what I believe, Major, it's the fact that I am trying to believe."

"And you really think you can win?"

"I can fight—and if I have weapons—well—yes, damn it, I could win!"

Major Kaufman got up and strode to the door. Opening it, he called out, "Orderly!" When the orderly came, Kaufman barked at him, "Didn't it ever occur to you to pick up the dishes?"

"But, Major, you're still drinking your tea."

"Don't give me that! Take that tray and get out of here!"

When the orderly had left, Adams lit another cigarette and watched Kaufman pace back and forth. It was very hot in the little office. The perspiration on Adams' face flowed down and wet his cigarette. Across Major Kaufman's shoulders a band of moisture darkened his shirt.

Then he stopped pacing and looked at Adams. "What do you want?" he asked.

"I want the report—and I want you as a witness for the defense."

"I'm glad you saved that until now."

"I wasn't certain that I wanted you as a witness until now."

"And now you are?"

"Yes."

"Give me a day or two to think it over."

"I can't give you an hour to think it over, Major," Barney Adams said stubbornly. "I have two days left to prepare my case. I can do it if I cut down my sleeping to a minimum. But I need your decision now."

"I suppose you know what it is?"

"I think so."

"Well, get out now. Get out and leave me alone. I have work to do, too, although you may not think so." He went to a metal filing case, opened a drawer, and took out a sheaf of paper. "Here's the report," he said.

"Thank you, sir."

"Ah, to hell with thanks! I'm not doing this for you, Adams."

"We convene at nine-thirty, Monday morning. At the Advocate's."

"All right. And don't bother—I know where it is."

Kaufman left the room, slamming the door behind him.

☆ Friday 3.10 P. M.

Half a dozen American correspondents and four British correspondents were already seated in General Kempton's big office when Barney Adams arrived. The general, who had a reputation as a stickler for punctuality, was in this instance remarkably genial and understanding. Before any questions were permitted, he spread his arms and told the newspapermen:

"I want you to understand that you are dealing with an infantry officer, not with your home-town mayor in uniform.

Major Alek Gunther is here from the PR office, and he knows the rules. You also know the rules. You can address any questions you wish to—to me or to Captain Adams. But if Major Gunther makes a no-comment decision, the decision holds. I don't want any arguments. And I don't want you buttonholing Captain Adams in the corridor for inside dope. There is no inside dope. This case is open—wide open."

And then turning to Gunther, "Do you have anything to add to that before we begin, Major?"

Gunther, slim, dark, impeccably tailored, his briefcase at the ready under his arm, as if prepared to step into a client's office, shook his head.

"You've covered it, General."

"Fire away," the general said.

The Associated Press man wanted to know whether Captain Adams had been brought into the theater specifically for this case.

"I wouldn't say that," the general answered, smiling. "He has been brought in because I wanted him on my staff."

From the *Times* man, "What do you think are your chances of saving Winston's life, Captain Adams?"

"I have no idea, nor do I have enough time to speculate on my chances. I was assigned to defend Lieutenant Winston. I shall do that to the best of my ability."

"Do you intend to enter a plea of insanity?" a British correspondent demanded.

"I'm afraid I cannot disclose my strategy before the court convenes," Adams replied.

The door to the office opened now, and a reporter for the major local paper entered. Dark, abashed, his white cotton clothes wrapped so strangely and gracefully about him, he remained standing next to the door at the back of the room. Gunther looked at him and said nothing.

A question came without Barney Adams' hearing it. He was wondering why he should doubt himself as he pointed to an empty chair and said to the native reporter, "Won't you please sit down, sir."

General Kempton watched Adams shrewdly. The native correspondent nodded his thanks as he gingerly and uncertainly went to the chair and sat down.

The *Manchester Guardian* correspondent then asked, "What is your opinion about the political issues involved here?"

"No comment on that. None." Major Gunther appeared pleased to make his firm hand felt. "This is a military trial, and there are no political issues involved."

"Oh, do be a bit flexible," protested the *Guardian* man. "Our readers are not concerned with how Winston is defended. They want to know the American attitude toward the murder of a British non-com."

"There is no comment on that," Gunther repeated. "You know the ground rules here."

The United Press man said, "General, could you intervene? I think it's a fair question. It cuts to the core of things. Editorials stateside are calling this a hot potato, not because a man murdered someone, but because an American officer murdered a British non-com."

"It's a hell of a broad question." Kempton smiled. "You can't just ask one's opinion of political issues involved. That covers too much. I think Barney Adams is a damn good lawyer. But he's not a congressman."

This fetched a laugh all around. Adams' respect for Kempton was increasing. He used his indolent, apparently good-natured bulk cleverly and well—and gave little indication of what lay beneath it. Yet at the same time there were clues to the man. Angry, he would be dangerous beyond expectation. So Adams thought, telling himself not to underestimate this man, not even to fall into the trap of taking him lightly.

Meanwhile, the native correspondent had come to his feet and was waiting to ask a question. Unlike the others, he did not speak out. He waited to be recognized, to be asked. Gunther ignored him, but Kempton nodded at him and said, "Go ahead, sir."

"About the political consequences," the man began, his English stilted, strangely accented, "I think that you are right to say that this is a very broad topic. For not only the murderer, but the hangman too, functions in terms of two peoples. My readers—"

Gunther cut in, "If you have a question, ask it. This is not a forum."

"I was merely trying to explain, sir, that my readers would ask this question—is there any justice apart from might? Can there be such justice?"

Gunther hesitated, unsure of himself now that the focus had been narrowed.

General Kempton said, not unkindly, "Who do you direct that at, Captain Adams or myself?"

"Captain Adams, sir, since he stands for the defense."

Watching the man, Adams thought again of the different worlds that Kaufman had specified. This man did not stand upright; out of training and habit, his muscles had lost the ability to hold him fully upright in the presence of white men. His knees were bent just a trifle, his shoulders bent just a trifle, his neck bowed just a trifle—even as his voice was muted, the words and meaning separated from the tone, which was carefully calculated not to give offense.

"I think," Adams answered slowly, "that justice can only exist apart from might. A result provided by power and necessity does not lie within my definition of justice."

He felt pompous and foolish after that reply, yet facing the man as he was, he didn't know what else he might have said.

The press conference went on, but the dark-skinned reporter did not ask any other questions.

☆ Friday 5:00 P.M.

When the press conference had finished, General Kempton asked Adams to remain for a few minutes. Adams sat down gratefully, exhausted in every bone and muscle of his body. General Kempton, observing him thoughtfully, asked if he had ever been the focus of a press conference before.

"No, sir," Adams replied. "This is the first time. May I smoke?"

"Help yourself, Barney." He lit the cigarette for Adams, and added, "Being shot up and cited never gave you anything like this. It takes a murder case."

Adams nodded, drawing on the cigarette with pleasure. He stared across the room.

"Done in?" the general asked.

"Yes, sir. I've been doing a lot of thinking. I'm not used to that."

"And what have you been thinking?"

"One thing and another. I've been thinking, sir, that I have killed better than twenty men—but I'll never stand trial for it, will I?"

"That's a hell of a note, Barney," the general said lightly. "You're the last man on earth I'd pick to go bitter on me."

"I'm not bitter, sir. Just tired."

"Out here a man goes stale quickly, if he allows it. Don't allow it, Barney. You've been too much with yourself."

"That's a question of time, sir."

"Barney, believe me, I know just how little time you have to dig into this thing. But you know you can't cram twenty-four hours a day for an exam. There's a point of saturation—then waste. Now look, tomorrow night there's a senior officers' dance at the mess barracks. There's a fine four-piece combination that flew in from Africa—anyway, they tell me it's good. There'll be some pretty girls and good company. I want you there."

Adams shook his head. "No—I can't, sir."

"You can and you will."

"Look, sir, I have to put my case together. I have two days to do a week's work. I just can't."

"I'm going to see you there, Barney. I'm going to insist. And look here—do you really believe you can bring Winston off?"

"I believe I've got a fighting chance, sir."

The general sat down behind his desk and drummed on the wood with his fingers. Then, without looking at Adams, he said, "Don't put your hopes too high."

"It's not a question of hopes, sir."

"No? What then?"

"I have a case. I'm not empty-handed, sir."

"I didn't think you'd go into court empty-handed, Barney. I just—well, you're taking this damned seriously."

"Shouldn't I, sir? Didn't you take it seriously when you brought me into it?"

"Yes, yes, of course I did. I want a defense put up, a good one. But damn it to hell, you're defending a confessed murderer!"

"I'm aware of that, sir."

"All right."

"Is that all, sir?" Adams asked.

"All?" Kempton asked—as if he had only just noticed Barney Adams. "Yes, I suppose so. Unless you need something. Don't hesitate to ask."

"I think I've been well provided." Adams smiled, rising.

"Good. And I like the way you handled yourself today."

"Thank you, sir. I think I did the Scout Movement credit."

"Hell, Barney," the general said, getting up and coming around his desk, "you always were something of a Boy Scout. But don't play it too earnestly with me, because the truth of it is we're neither of us as stupid or simple as we act." He put one arm around Adams' shoulders and said, "God damn it, I'd give up these silly stars and a year or two of my life too—just to have been the regimental commander who had your company in his outfit."

For the first time it occurred to Barney Adams that he was beginning to dislike General Kempton.

☆ Saturday 3.18 A.M.

Barney Adams awakened out of the dream; and he lay there in his bed under the mosquito netting, his pajamas damp to his body, the night heat clammy and oppressive. It occurred to him, as such things do, that he might find a moment to tell Major Kaufman about his dream. He had heard that dreams reproduce the incidents of life only symbolically, but this dream was not symbolic. He dreamed it over and over, and each time he was dreaming about something that had happened. Even during the dream, a part of himself knew that the thing had happened, and he felt a sort of resentment when the dream departed from or changed the original reality.

He would dream about Gabowski's mother, whom he had never seen, and he knew that part was contrivance. For Gabowski's mother, Adams in his dream created a short, stout, gray-haired woman with a sweet face and watery blue eyes. She wore an apron of yellow and white checked material, and she was always cooking as he saw her, beating eggs or mixing a cake or scraping fish. For some reason he had decided that fish was a favorite food in Gabowski's home, perhaps because when he himself was a child they almost never had fish on their table, perhaps because Gabowski's background had to be so different from his own.

Howsoever, each time he dreamed he made the same mother for Gabowski, until she became so familiar and real that he half believed in her, and wondered whether or not Gabowski had shown him a picture of the woman. If Gabowski had shown him such a picture, Adams could not recall the occasion; but this did not surprise him. He knew that he had developed the ability to forget things he did not desire to remember.

On four different occasions Barney Adams had received letters from Mrs. Gabowski, and each time she had begged him not to tell Gabowski that she was writing to his company officer. She knew about her son's sensitivities, and was as careful as she could be not to cause him embarrassment. She wrote a painful scrawl, was a poor speller, and did strange things with a language she had not been born to, but with all this there was somehow in her letters an almost courtly grace and perception that moved Adams deeply. Each letter ended with a little blessing and prayer for Captain Adams' health and happiness. In the first letter, Mrs. Gabowski apologized for her presumption in offering the prayer, for she was a Catholic and she knew—perhaps in her mind she classified all commissioned officers so—that Captain Adams was a Protestant. But when Adams wrote back thanking her for the prayer, she made no further reference to the matter.

It was not until the fourth letter, evidently, that Mrs. Gabowski felt sufficiently comfortable in their acquaintance to bring up the matter of the vitamins. She informed Barney Adams, with many apologies, that she had taken the great liberty of sending to him, under separate cover, a bottle of 500 Unicaps. Her handwriting became even worse as she begged him to do something she had no right to ask, to see that Gabowski took a vitamin tablet every day. She explained how much this would mean to both herself and her son, and she also explained that it would have done her no good to have sent the bottle directly to Gabowski. He would be ashamed to carry a bottle of vitamins with him, and he would throw it away first chance he had.

Barney Adams knew that this was so. Gabowski was a round-faced, pink-cheeked boy of nineteen years. He was short, chubby, and gentle as a lamb. Where the other men grew respectable black and brown and red whiskers in the rain and mud and foxholes, Gabowski put forth a colorless, soft stubble. Where the other men smoked whatever they could lay hands on, Gabowski went into a fit of coughing every time he lit a cigarette. And the one time Gabowski got drunk on red wine, he passed out and had to be carried back to the company area.

Adams was trapped. There was no way out. Day after day, bound by the silence of honor and duty beyond the call of duty which a woman had placed upon him, he had to find Gabowski and, with threats and rank, force him to take a vitamin pill.

There was the night in Italy when he crawled up to Lieutenant Jacob's position and said, "Where in hell's name is that God damned Gabowski?"

Adams guarded a secret that was no secret at all. The lieutenant kept a straight face as he told Adams that their line to artillery had been cut somewhere, and Gabowski and Winnaker had gone out along the line to repair it.

"They'll be back in a few minutes, I think, sir. Why don't you wait?" the lieutenant asked.

"I'll go along the line," Adams said, and he started off, bending low, running the line through his gloved fingers. The vitamins bulged in his pocket.

It was very quiet at first. Adams was moving back, and he had just decided to walk upright when some shelling began. He dropped to his face. There were only four rounds. Then he crawled along the wire and his outstretched hand touched a face. He knew it was Gabowski's face, and it was upside down, as if Gabowski were standing on his head.

Adams began to tremble. He pulled off a glove, but his hand was shaking so that he could hardly put it into his pocket to get out his lighter. When the lighter flared, he saw the wet red stump of Gabowski's neck, the head imbedded in the mud on its silky yellow hair.

When he dreamed, it was at this moment that he awakened, leaving this final recollection etched sharply and precisely. Now, under the mosquito netting, he rolled over onto his stomach, put his face in the pillow, and began to cry.

☆ *Saturday 8.40 P.M.*

At the mess barracks, Barney Adams said to Corporal Baxter, "Do you have a date tonight, Corporal?"

"I got a sort of tomato at Conga Flats. She's good for tonight."

"Take the jeep and enjoy yourself."

Baxter protested. He had developed a half-protective attitude toward the captain, and wanted to know how Adams would get home.

"I'll pick up a ride. Take off."

The barracks was brightly lit, the tables rearranged to form a good-sized dance floor. The four-piece combination from back home was very good indeed, and when Barney Adams entered, it was playing "South of the Border." The song had always produced a sentimental reaction in him; it was like hearing "There's a Long, Long Trail A-Winding," which went much further back but touched him the same way.

For a while, Adams stood just inside the big screen doors, watching the officers enter with their dates, Red Cross women and nurses and a sprinkling of girls from the British families in residence. He had the lonely and restive feeling of a man who comes alone to a dance and knows that he will be alone through the evening, and he had half made up his mind to stay no more than fifteen or twenty minutes and then leave. He nodded and spoke a few words to officers he had been introduced to and to men he knew by sight from the Makra Palace.

One or two of them said, "I'll buy you a drink, Captain."

He nodded and put it off. There was no real bar, but a great bowl of gin-spiked punch had been set up on a table at the other end of the room, and already it held its own circle of earnest drinkers. A dozen or so couples were on the floor; because of the heat, they cut the time in two as they moved.

Behind him, a woman said, "Good evening, Captain Adams."

Nothing could have astonished Barney Adams more. He turned and saw the nurse who had berated him in Major Kaufman's office the day before. She had added make-up to her dress uniform and she was smiling. It made a difference.

"You have a nice smile, Lieutenant," he said.

103

"So have you, Captain Adams. My name is Kate Sorenson—so please don't call me Lieutenant."

"Very well, Miss Sorenson. My name is Barney Adams."

"So I understand."

"Well—yes. Of course." He stood there and looked past her.

"I have no date tonight, if that's what you're looking for. A group of us came up from the hospital. I came along. I'm surprised to find you here, I will say that."

"Why?"

"I don't know. I just didn't think you would be here."

"I'm surprised to hear that you thought about it at all."

"Well, there you are." She shrugged. "I hope it's a pleasant surprise for both of us."

"It's very pleasant for me," Adams said. "I was beginning to feel sorry for myself. I don't like to feel sorry for myself."

"You don't permit yourself much sentiment, do you, Captain?"

"Only what I can handle, Miss Sorenson."

"And do you have contempt for people who lose their temper—as I did yesterday?"

"No—no, I don't," Adams replied reflectively. "I'm sure you had good reason to defend Major Kaufman. He's an extraordinary man."

"What are you trying to say, Captain?" she asked sharply. "Do you think I'm his girl?"

"I didn't say that, did I?"

"Let me make it plain that I am not."

"Please, I didn't mean to offend you. Understand me—I don't care what relationship exists between you and Major Kaufman." He shook his head then. "No, that's not it. This is a bad night for me, Miss Sorenson. I felt lonely and miser-

104

able before you said hello to me. I wanted to hear what you just said."

"A nurse sometimes has a peculiar kind of hero worship," Lieutenant Sorenson said. "When you work with a man like Major Kaufman, you can become involved with him—but not that way. I'm not talking about myself. He just wasn't having any."

"It's none of my business." He looked at her suspiciously. "What changed your feeling about me, Miss Sorenson?"

"He did."

"I brought him trouble," Adams said.

"He had trouble. Maybe you brought him something else."

"Maybe. I don't know."

She was watching him searchingly, and he wondered: What does she see and what is she thinking? Do I show her how much I need someone to be with and talk to tonight?

"I read all about you," she said simply. "It was in today's paper. I read that you were one of the heroes of the North African campaign, and that you are a brave and honorable man." She said this with no note of scorn or sarcasm, but directly, as if she knew quite well how old-fashioned and embarrassing her statement was.

"There aren't any heroes," he answered, almost sorrowfully.

"What did you do to make the man who wrote about you feel the way he did?" she asked. "His name is Sundar Jatee, and he has a reputation for cynicism and clever hatred when it comes to the British or us."

"I asked him to sit down," Adams remembered.

☆ *Saturday 10.45 P.M.*

They had been dancing, and Adams was hot and wet and a little tight from five glasses of the punch. Kate Sorenson had matched his drinking, but she held it well. She took him by the arm, firmly, and led him out into the gardens behind the barracks. A sweet, pungent smell was thick as honey in the air.

"What am I smelling, Kate?" he wanted to know.

"Jasmine."

"I was out here after lunch but there was no smell."

"You only smell the jasmine at night. It gives off its odor then, but I don't know why."

They sat down on an old stone bench. There was a yellow moon in the sky. The faintest whisper of a breeze cooled them a bit. From behind the screen doors, the four-piece combination was playing a medley from *The Student Prince*.

"They wouldn't play numbers like that stateside," Sorenson remarked. "I guess they learned somewhere that they get a big hand for nostalgia."

"My father and mother saw the show. When my father had a leave, they'd go to New York and buy tickets for everything that was playing. If it was a musical, my mother would buy the sheet music. Then she'd work it out on the piano. It took a lot of patience because she wasn't the world's best pianist, but I remember that I would sit and watch her and be convinced that she was. We would sing the songs together."

"You must have had a happy childhood, Barney."

"I suppose so. It seems ordinary when I look back. I was an only child. I wanted to measure up to what my father expected and I never felt that I did."

"What did he expect?"

"It wasn't what he expected. It was what I thought he expected. I was always afraid of him. Look at the moon, Kate."

"Oh, the hell with the moon and this stinking jasmine! The hell with you, too, Barney! What kind of a damn fool am I to be sitting here and waiting for you to romance me?"

"I don't know," he shrugged. "There are all kinds of damn fools, Kate—your kind, my kind."

"Why don't you make a pass—or do you time things? When is the proper moment? Don't sit there with your mouth full of teeth, like a damn collar ad! This is it. We're at war, and all that West Point and warm, sweet childhood and mother at the piano picking out the melodies will now pay off. You'll be a general if it lasts long enough."

"Who are you defending now?" he asked quietly.

"Myself."

"All right—if you have to."

"Yes, I have to."

"Do you want to tell me why?"

"Don't pull the sympathy act, Barney. You don't know a damn thing—not one damn thing. What does war teach you— how to die? It's more important to know how to live. I'm as lonely as you are, but it doesn't warm the cockles of my heart to sit here and listen to your happy childhood and think about

107

what a fine, clean-cut American boy Barney Adams is. My mother came here from Sweden in 1916, and I was born two months after she arrived. Mr. Sorenson never came. My mother was a cleaning woman in the biggest office building in Minneapolis, and I was knocked over and laid when I was fifteen years old. I became a nurse the way Max Kaufman became a doctor, by cutting a little piece of my heart out each day and depositing it at the First National Bank, and I always felt I was rich until now."

Barney Adams was watching her. She sat unmoving and fixed in her own woe. Like that, the two of them sat there, and minutes went by, until at last she whispered, "Get in your jeep, Captain, and go home."

"I sent the jeep away, Kate," he said matter-of-factly. "They gave me this Corporal Baxter as a driver, and at first I just felt that I would like to see him bleed to death slowly, because he was that kind of a guy. But then I got kind of fond of him, and he had a date tonight. So I told him to take the jeep."

"You're noble. You're so damned brave and noble."

"If I'd known that I'd have a date," he said apologetically, "I wouldn't have been so noble."

"You don't have a date. Go home."

"No. You see, the trouble with people like Kaufman and yourself is that while you put up a great front about being sorry for yourselves, you're not sorry at all. In fact, you are as imperious as hell and you look down on anyone who has been handed anything. I had a top sergeant in my company who was the biggest bookie in Philadelphia before he became a sergeant. He was a good infantry sergeant, with imagination and resourcefulness, but because he had made it before he was thirty years old, he treated his men with contempt and trusted them no further than he could throw them. I had to break him from his rank, but that only fixed his opinion of people like me. Well, you—"

"Stop that!" she cried.

"I was only trying to explain why I'm not going home. You can't send me away, Kate."

He put an arm around her shoulder, and she said, "Make your pass, soldier. A nurse is open season. Haven't you heard of nurses who banked fifty grand in areas where women were in short supply?"

"I hear all kind of things, Kate."

Then she put her head down against his shoulder and remained silent.

☆ Sunday 12.20 A.M.

The moon had turned silver and flooded the sleeping city with its light. The rickshaw boy moved at a slow trot that was almost a walk, and the scent of the night lay on them. The whole feeling of Barney Adams was of being alive; he had never been alive like this before, inside and outside, aware of himself and his soul and being and beginning and end, but without fear or the trouble of time; and also aware of the woman who sat next to him. He knew how good it was to be alive, how gracious and sweet.

He savored the smells of the night. The city was full of smells, jasmine carried on the wind and the smell of burnt charcoal and the smell of decay and the smell of man and the smell of the jungle and the salty far-off promise of the monsoon. He savored all the smells and used them as a part of his being. His being alive was a part of his will and urgency—and he sensed that the whole world was for man to know and use and comprehend.

"Haven't you a girl at home?" she asked him softly.

"No."

"Half of the world is women. Why didn't any of them love you?"

"Because I didn't love any of them, I suppose. Because I wasn't looking for love."

"I don't believe that two people can fall in love like this. Not two people as far apart as you and me."

"If it happens, it doesn't matter whether or not you believe it."

"I can't live in a dream."

"I've been living in a dream," Adams said. "I woke up tonight. I know who I am and I know who you are."

"Who are we, Barney?"

"We're people. We're filled with life and compassion—and we're connected with all the time that was and all the time that will be."

"Oh, you're a strange man," she said. "You say things that no one else would say, and you're untroubled. I never knew anyone as untroubled as you are, Barney Adams. When I was in training, I met boys who looked like you. I hated them. They were empty."

"I was empty," he said.

"I don't believe that."

"I knew I was empty. That made a difference."

"I don't understand that."

"I know. I'm trying to say a lot of things tonight that I never said before, and I don't know how to say them. I haven't had any practice. Look"—he pointed to the rickshaw boy—"can't we walk? I can't sit here and talk and have him pulling me like that. How far is it?"

"Not far. Less than a mile."

They stopped the rickshaw and paid the man. Then they walked through the night, Barney Adams holding her hand.

When they came to the hospital, she turned to him and said, "Everything else is all right, and I guess I'm as happy as I have ever been in all my life, but don't say that you're in love with me. You don't have to say that—I swear you don't. Because you're not in love with me, and I am not in love with you. You can have me or any part of me or anything that I own. That's the way I am. I'm not like the girls you knew over stateside—like the girls at the West Point Ball that you were telling me about."

"What are they like, Kate?"

"You know—it has to be signed, sealed and delivered. Jesus Christ, Barney, stop playing games with me!"

"I'm not playing games with you, Kate."

"Barney, Barney," she whispered, "why are you making it so hard for me? I don't want anything. I'll take tonight. And tomorrow night, if you want it that way. When it's done, it's done."

"You want it that way? Tell me why, Kate."

"Because there isn't any other way."

"You don't believe I love you?"

"No, I don't believe it."

☆ Sunday 10.00 A.M.

Barney Adams was eating his breakfast in the dining room
of the Makra Palace, a room of blue and white and yellow tile
that reminded him of Sanborn's in Mexico City, when two
young men approached his table. He invited them to sit down
and join him for coffee, and they introduced themselves as
Lieutenants Harvey Bender and Oscar Moscow. They would
be delighted to have coffee with him, they said, because it
was common knowledge that the coffee here was the only
coffee in the city that was fit to drink—except of course for
the Turkish coffee which they prepared in the Hotel Imperial.

But they said this with diffidence, and they obviously
regarded Captain Adams with some awe. They were intelli-
gent-looking young men, both of them in their early twenties,
Bender towheaded and tall and thin, Moscow nearsighted,
quietly intent behind his glasses.

"It's my fault that we're meeting only now," Barney Adams
said as he shook hands with them. "I should have seen you
Friday at the latest, but nothing in this case is ordinary. I had
to use every moment."

"Please don't apologize, sir," Lieutenant Bender protested.
"We understand the circumstances."

"I don't want you to feel that I am deprecating my assist-

112

ants. I knew that you two men were to assist me. I value such assistance beyond measure."

"Thank you," Lieutenant Bender said.

"Perhaps I'm talking out of turn," Lieutenant Moscow put in, "but I have never heard of a refusal to grant a continuance in a capital case. Not where defense counsel has been arbitrarily changed. I suppose you know, sir, that it was not Winston who demanded new counsel."

"I know that."

"Then how on earth can they deny a continuance?" Bender demanded.

"Now wait a moment," Adams told them. "They haven't denied any delay because I haven't asked for any. I haven't asked for a continuance because I was plainly given to understand that I should not ask for one—that this case must be delayed no longer."

"Why, that's outrageous!"

"It is not outrageous," Adams said quietly. "A court-martial must sublimate itself to military necessity—which, like it or not, is the prime necessity of a nation at war."

"Then what happens to the whole concept of trial justice?" Moscow wanted to know.

"It exists—not as it does in civilian courts, but within a certain frame of reference. And, let me assure you, our frame of reference is the most just of any on earth. You were both civilian lawyers?"

They nodded.

"Then you must lay aside certain things that you accepted unconditionally. I don't think we want a continuance. I go before officers whom I must convince. I think I can convince them better at this moment than at a later moment."

"This is good coffee," Bender said. "I guess I haven't had

113

such good coffee since I'm here. Do you mind if I have a roll with it, Captain?"

"Go right ahead."

"It's funny, the only day I have an appetite for breakfast is Sunday. You don't raise much of an appetite in this heat." He buttered a roll and heaped marmalade on it.

Moscow's brow was creased. "Sir?"

"Yes, Lieutenant?"

"I can't say that I follow that. Why do you feel that you can convince them better now?"

"Because they have no doubts at this moment—no doubts at all. They know that Winston murdered Quinn. They will go through the formality of a court-martial because it is required of them, but they don't know of any reason why Winston should not hang."

"I must say that I don't know any reason," Bender said, his mouth full of roll.

"There you are."

"Sir?"

"You see," Adams explained, "where there is no doubt, there is no defense against doubt. There was a young fellow from the Georgia hills in my company. He was a fundamentalist, and never in his life had he questioned or doubted his convictions. Then one day he got into a discussion with a couple of freethinkers in the company and they tore his fundamentalism to shreds. He went to pieces. He had no defense against doubt, no experience with doubt."

"But is that a fair comparison?" Moscow wondered.

"No, of course not. But it does deal with the question of doubt. If I force a delay, doubts will appear, because this case is full of doubt. Arguments will create counter-arguments,

114

and my own case will be weakened. Anyway, I am not sure that time will gain us anything."

"You mean the case can't be won under any circumstances?"

"I don't mean that at all," Adams said. "But suppose we finish our breakfast."

☆ Sunday 10.40 A.M.

Lieutenant Bender was still drinking coffee and eating rolls when Lieutenant Moscow brought out the diagram of the court-martial. Lieutenant Bender was a natural eater; he ate quickly, competently and professionally, without lingering to savor taste or quality. While Bender ate, Lieutenant Moscow explained that Colonel Thompson, the Judge Advocate General, had sent his apologies along with the diagram.

"Strictly off the record, sir," said Moscow, "his apologies don't mean a thing. You should have had the diagram yesterday at the latest, and if I weren't discussing my CO, I would—"

"But you are discussing your CO," Adams pointed out. "I think we must get one thing straight and hold to it. There is no conspiracy here. No one is out to get defense counsel. We recognize that the theater command wishes to hang Winston and get it over with. They feel that there is reason to

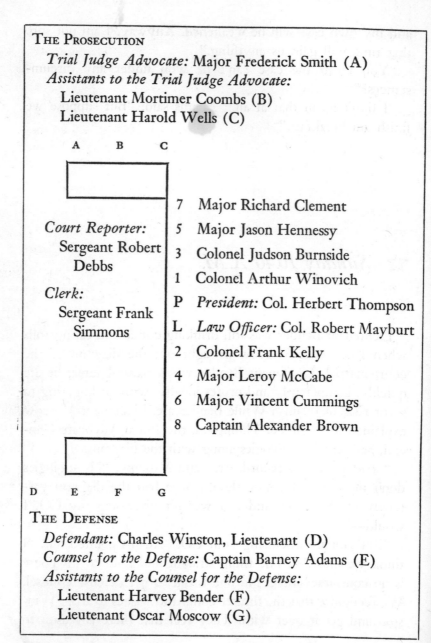

THE PROSECUTION

Trial Judge Advocate: Major Frederick Smith (A)
Assistants to the Trial Judge Advocate:
Lieutenant Mortimer Coombs (B)
Lieutenant Harold Wells (C)

A   B   C

	7 Major Richard Clement
Court Reporter:	5 Major Jason Hennessy
Sergeant Robert Debbs	3 Colonel Judson Burnside
	1 Colonel Arthur Winovich
Clerk:	P *President:* Col. Herbert Thompson
Sergeant Frank Simmons	L *Law Officer:* Col. Robert Mayburt
	2 Colonel Frank Kelly
	4 Major Leroy McCabe
	6 Major Vincent Cummings
	8 Captain Alexander Brown

D   E   F   G

THE DEFENSE

Defendant: Charles Winston, Lieutenant (D)
Counsel for the Defense: Captain Barney Adams (E)
Assistants to the Counsel for the Defense:
Lieutenant Harvey Bender (F)
Lieutenant Oscar Moscow (G)

116

hang him, and that with his death they will accomplish certain things. I think they are wrong, and I am going to prove that they are wrong. There is the virtue of our way of life—if you care to think of such a thing as virtue—that I can confront them, challenge them, and stop them. Petty annoyances are meaningless. The only meaningful thing is the verdict."

"He's right," Bender said.

"Yes, sir," Moscow agreed, catching some of the other's enthusiasm. Pointing to the diagram, he added, "Whatever the verdict is—it's in their hands."

"Good. Now let us get down to cases, gentlemen. We'll start with the prosecution. First of all, Major Smith."

Bender chewed his contempt with the food. "He's nothing. Nothing, sir."

"For God's sake," Moscow said, "stop eating, Harvey. All you've done is eat since we met the captain. What kind of an impression does it make?"

"I'm sorry—really sorry, sir."

"I'd love to see you fill up." Adams told him. "I give you my word, Bender, we'll do it again. About Major Smith?"

"Well," Moscow said, "it's easy to underestimate him. You understand, Captain Adams, we will have to talk frankly. Could we say in effect that this conversation is privileged?"

"Of course it's privileged," Adams agreed.

"In that case, we can start by saying that Major Smith is a boob. You agree, Harvey?"

"Right."

"But you can underestimate him just because he is a boob. He's a partner in a big Wall Street firm—corporation law, and that impresses people. He has a good memory and he knows a lot of law, but unless I'm mistaken, he has no criminal trial experience at all. Is that so, Harvey?"

"None," said Bender. "I checked that point because I knew, you'd be asking me, Captain. He's been after Colonel Thompson to give him a big trial job because he wants to get his name in the papers and impress his partners. And because of his position at home, sir, Colonel Thompson will brown-nose him right down the line, if you'll forgive the expression."

"I'll forgive it, but find another one."

"Harvey," Moscow said patiently, "Captain Adams is in a peculiar position here. Try to remember."

"Just say what you want to say," Adams told them. "Don't worry about me. The important thing is to fill in the holes. Now about Smith—can he think on his feet?"

"He doesn't have to," Bender said. "He's got Morty Coombs sitting behind him."

"Lieutenant Coombs," Adams repeated, staring at the diagram. "What about him?"

"Twenty-two years old, *summa cum laude*, City College of New York, first five, NYU Law School, stinking little genius, total retention, knows more military law at this point than anyone in the world—"

"Look up the captain's record, Harvey, before you go overboard. Sure, Morty Coombs is smart. But he's no diplomat. You've got to be more than a genius to infuse Major Smith with intelligence. If Smith had humility, he'd use Coombs, but Smith doesn't know how. Do you think he's going to take tactics from a snotty twenty-two-year-old lieutenant? Do you think Coombs can communicate with Smith? Maybe if he had doubts, but like the captain said, he doesn't have doubts."

"All right," Adams said. "Now what about Lieutenant Wells?"

"Just don't write Morty Coombs off," Bender insisted.

"I'm not writing him off. I'm simply trying to give the captain a balanced picture. You see, sir? Harold Wells, on the other hand, is a horse of another color entirely. Wells was an assistant D.A. in Boston. Thirty-three years old, Harvey?"

"Thirty-four, Harvard Law School, Beacon Hill, lots of money in the family, Late George Apley type."

"To answer your question, sir," Moscow said, "Smith can't think on his feet—Harold Wells can. He knows how to try a case, good presence, fine Boston accent. Smith is a plodder; Wells is a jabbing fighter—you know, with the left all the time. But Major Smith knows that, and he'd die before he'd let Wells in."

"It would be a hell of a team without Smith," Bender commented, grinning.

"We'll come back to them," Adams suggested. "Let's talk about the court. Start with the president. I met Colonel Thompson. Are my impressions of him correct?"

Bender waited while Moscow searched Barney Adams' placid face shrewdly. "You try a case that way, Captain?" Moscow asked.

"When it's called for."

"Your impressions are correct," Moscow admitted.

"Now, off the record and privileged, gentlemen—I am somewhat surprised to see the Judge Advocate General as the president of the court. It's done, but poorly done, I think, and bad practice. Why?"

"He couldn't resist," Bender shrugged. "How could he resist?"

"If I may say so, sir," Moscow added, "no infantry officer understands the fine points of publicity."

"Leave it at that," Adams agreed.

119

"If I may say so, sir," Moscow put in, "there is one man Colonel Thompson is afraid of. No, that isn't the word. Not fear, but respect. I mean, no nonsense. And that's our one real break on this diagram—Colonel Mayburt, the law officer. If Colonel Mayburt says it's law, it is law, depend on that, Captain."

"Tell me about him."

"Late forties," Bender said, "I think, forty-nine. Tall, handsome man. Lewis Stone type—you remember the Andy Hardy pictures?"

Adams nodded.

"Judge Hardy, in the flesh. But not corny—he was a judge in Elizabeth, New Jersey, criminal court. Eleven years. District Attorney, six years. Beautiful wife, seven children, Board of Directors, First National Bank of Middle Jersey. When he was D.A. he broke the Owney Gleason mob, right through Essex and Hudson counties. Incorruptible. He had it out, showdown stuff, with Hague, and he walked back to his own corner. I tell you, Captain, a man with a record like that ought to be President or at least a senator. Instead, he enlists in the army and lets himself be sent out here to this ass-hole of creation."

"How do you know all this?" Adams asked in amazement.

"I keep myself posted," Bender replied modestly. "Oscar and I have some talent. Not what you deserve, but some."

"About Colonel Mayburt," Moscow said, "he will deal law, sir, good, solid law. You can be sure of your ground. He'll never pull the rug from under you."

"That's good to know."

"I imagined you'd like that, sir."

"I do. Now let's go to the court itself. We'll move across the diagram. Major Clement first."

120

"Maybe a year or two older than you, Captain. Regular Army man—very quiet. He listens. Very serious, and so far as we can find out, no expression of opinion on the Winston case."

"Major Hennessy?"

"Ah!" Bender nodded. "He used to be a cop on the New York City force. Studied law. Self-made. He would be for guilty, hands down, but he hates the British."

"He doesn't just hate them," Moscow added; "his father was an Irishman who was killed in this Black and Tan business. It makes for an opening."

"Colonel Burnside?"

"No brains, none at all. He's a southern gentleman with fine manners and very agreeable. How can you measure such a man? He will agree with you. He will agree with Smith. He will also agree with Thompson."

"Colonel Winovich?"

"Guilty. He's a corporation lawyer from Pittsburgh. He won't even listen very much."

"Colonel Kelly?"

"He's a nice fellow—doesn't hate anyone. But he feels that hanging's too good for Winston."

"Major McCabe?"

"He think Winston ought to be shot and hanged both. An infantry officer like yourself. Hard as nails, but the boys who served under him in Burma worship the ground he walks on."

"Major Cummings?"

"Air Force. He's only twenty-six years old, and he has a wonderful record. Shot down over the jungle twice, and walked out each time. They say he's not afraid of anything on earth, including General Kempton. As far as we can find out,

121

he knows very little about the case. The trouble is, he's been dating a British girl."

"So our spies tell us," Moscow said. "But who knows on what basis a man dates a girl? The fact is that Cummings has an independent mind—nothing frozen. He will listen to reason."

"And Captain Brown?"

"I think they wanted company rank on the court," Moscow said. "My guess is that they deliberately omitted anyone of general rank for the same reason that they brought you to the defense, Captain—because the cards are stacked against Winston and because this has become a sort of general headache in Washington and London and everywhere else. They want to have a sort of jury of peers, so as to speak. Captain Brown is from supply, just as Winston was. He's a sort of white-collar officer, like Bender here and myself, and he certainly won't fight city hall."

"He's a man of no distinction." Bender nodded agreement.

"At least," Adams said, "I have background knowledge now. Suppose we go into the lounge and find a quiet corner and get to work."

"But what about your challenges, sir?" Bender wanted to know. "We have a replacement list of seventeen officers. Don't you want to go through them?"

"No. I'm not going to use any challenges."

Bender was shocked. He appeared to feel that he and all his vast statistical and investigatory knowledge had been summarily rejected. "I'm afraid I don't follow you, Captain," he said with great dignity.

"Come, Lieutenant," Barney Adams said kindly, "let's see just what a challenge is. The civilian lawyer sets great stock by them, because he has a set of rules for externalizing a

122

person's character. I don't believe in such rules. I don't know very much about any person—not even myself—and when I make a judgment, as often as not it turns out to be wrong.

"Now, I have one peremptory challenge. If I exercise it, I risk the hostility of the entire court. I am a soldier first—I can't forget that. Now, as to challenge for cause—do you know what it means to specify cause when dealing with superior officers?"

Bender shook his head. Moscow said slowly, "Do you know, I think he's right, Harvey."

☆ *Monday 8.30 A.M.*

The building which housed the Judge Advocate General was a former governmental residence. Strangely enough, in that subtropical land, it was built in the late Georgian style, and surrounded by a brick wall with wrought-iron gates. It was said that all the bricks for its construction had been brought by sailing ship from England at great cost, which Adams could believe, there being so few brick buildings in the city. The building had fine proportions, and it was the one building in the city that filled Adams and many other Americans with nostalgia, for it was not unlike many buildings at home.

When the building was first turned over to the U.S. Command, it was in poor shape and had not been in use for several years. By now, it had been repaired and the rotting wood had been replaced or painted; and as Barney Adams saw it at half-past eight this Monday morning, the sunlight falling upon its tiled roof and old red walls, the palm trees bending over it, the hibiscus against its brick walls, it made a pleasant sight. It seemed incongruous that a murder trial would take place here.

"Well, sir," said Corporal Baxter as the jeep went through the gates, "this is it, isn't it? Zero hour."

A certain affection had overlaid Baxter's initial dislike, and he was protective toward Adams. "Anything I can do, just name it, Captain," he said as he parked the jeep.

"I'm afraid all you can do is sit around and wait, Baxter. I wish I could give you the day off, but I can't take a chance on needing the jeep and not having it here."

"Don't give it a second thought, Captain. I like to sit. And I want to wish you good luck. It's a hell of a note that they got to go to such lengths because someone knocked over a limey."

At that moment General Kempton's car, driven by Sergeant Candyman, drew up. Kempton got out, followed by two of his staff officers, whom he introduced to Barney Adams.

"What do you think, Barney?" the general asked.

Adams shrugged. "I've done what I can. Now we'll see."

Half a dozen correspondents were already waiting as they entered the building. They surrounded the general's party, pleading for a break.

"Gentlemen, when have I ever refused to give you a break?"

"General, let us cover it on the inside."

Barney Adams realized that Kempton was not as unruffled

124

as he appeared to be. His face flushed as he snapped, "No! I won't even discuss that! You know it's impossible!"

Past the reporters, Adams saw Bender and Moscow talking to a thin, dyspeptic man who carried a briefcase under his arm. Bender caught his eye, and Adams walked over to them.

"Good morning, sir," Moscow said. "This is Trial Judge Advocate, Major Smith. Captain Adams, sir."

Major Smith accepted Adams tolerantly. "I hear you're going to make a good show of it, Captain."

"I hope to try."

"Good. It wouldn't do to just hang the poor devil."

"No, it wouldn't do at all, sir."

"Well, see you in the trenches," Smith said, taking off toward the reporters.

Bender whispered, "My Aunt Sadie—see you in the trenches! See what I mean, sir?"

One of the correspondents approached Adams. He recognized the Associated Press man who had been in Kempton's office. The correspondent wanted to know about the rumor that Adams would plead Winston's insanity.

"You know I can't divulge my plans."

"Let a word drop. Give us a lead."

Shaking his head, Kempton pushed between them, hooked his arm in Adams', and led him away.

"Come in here a moment, Barney," the general said, opening one of two tall white doors that faced the entrance hall. Adams followed, and the general closed the door behind them. They were in the court now, a room forty feet long and twenty-five feet wide, with six high windows facing them. Fans on the ceiling turned lazily. A long table of polished mahogany stretched full twenty feet, with ten chairs placed behind it. At either end, a smaller table was set at right angles, much as the diagram had depicted.

"Nice room, isn't it," the general observed, his mind obviously elsewhere.

"Very nice, sir."

"Barney," he said suddenly, "how far are you going to push this case?"

"To a point where I win it, sir."

"And you still think you can win?"

"Yes, sir, I do. I have a tough case here, but I think I also have a good case."

"The only case you have is an insanity plea."

"If Winston was insane when he murdered Quinn, then he is not guilty—is he, sir?"

"Let the court decide, Barney. You haven't the chance of a snowball in hell of proving insanity, and you know it."

"You may be right, sir."

"Oh, damn it all," the general said, putting his arm on Adams' shoulder, "why am I snapping at you, Barney? I brought you into this. All I want you to remember is that we are only interested in establishing a record that cannot be questioned. The man is a murderer. There's no doubt of that." The general spread his hands now. "You have no obligation to save his life, Barney—your only obligation is to defend him, to give him the use of guarantees provided by military justice."

"That is what I intend to do, sir."

"I wonder? Look, Barney, I'm going to level with you. The British Command here asked to be present. I had no alternative except to invite them. Then the Assistant to the Home Secretary in London decided to fly in quietly and take me by surprise. Of course, I had to invite him too. You'd think with

126

the way they've been pasted by bombs and with all their headaches in Italy that they would hardly be able to or want to stick their noses into this affair, but evidently this is in their tradition, and Winston and Quinn rate high there. A British M.P. comes down from the north at the same time—another guest. Now the U.S. Consul General here tells me that he would like to be present. I can't admit the British fellow and keep him out. So aside from myself and two staff members, we're going to have three civilians and six British brass—that's what those chairs at the end of the room are for.

"Now, Barney, I want you to know this."

"Thank you, sir. But it makes no difference as far as I am concerned."

"Doesn't it, Barney? How plain must I be?"

"Are you trying to tell me, sir—"

"Let's leave that unsaid," the general replied firmly. "I am advising nothing. I am telling you what the situation is. Do you understand me, Barney?"

"I think I understand you, sir," Barney Adams replied.

☆ *Monday 9.40 A.M.*

As Major Smith rose to make his opening statement, Barney Adams looked around the court and felt his pulse quicken and his throat tighten. For him, the court of military law was not

127

simply and merely the judicial process of the armed forces; it was the leaven of civilization thrust tentatively into that ancient instrument of death and destruction, the soldiery. It was the paradox out of which man's hope creeps and explores. It was also the arena in which he had chosen to play out a life which, beyond any possibility of youthful choice, was destined to be military.

He could not have wholly expressed how deeply the court moved him, the ten senior officers sitting sternly behind the long mahogany table, the prosecution at one end of the table, the defense at the other, the military policemen in all their dress-uniform show guarding the doors, the guests seated at the other end of the long room, among them a Scots officer in kilt and plaid, the flags banked between the high windows, the witnesses at the opposite end of the room, and the hot morning sunlight fighting through the crevices of the blinds.

He felt content and at peace with himself for the first time in many days.

"—and the Trial Judge Advocate will prove," Major Smith was saying, "that Charles Winston, Lieutenant in the Army of the United States, planned this murder deliberately, proceeded to it with forethought, and committed it while in full possession of all his faculties—"

Adams turned to look at Winston. The defendant sat slumped in his chair, examining the back of his fingernails, either indifferent to or unaware of what was happening around him. He expressed neither joy nor sorrow, nor was his skinny figure, clad in loose and faded fatigues, evocative of hatred or sympathy. It was almost as if he alone, the defendant, were not present, but only a word, a definition, a shadow of himself.

128

Colonel Thompson said, "Captain Adams, do you desire to make an opening statement?"

Adams rose. "If the court please, I have no opening statement to make. But if the court will hear me, I would like to make a request at this point."

"The court will hear you, sir."

"Then I would respectfully request that all witnesses except the witness whose testimony is being taken, be excluded from the courtroom. And that witnesses be called only to testify."

Colonel Thompson turned to Colonel Mayburt, the Law Officer seated on his left. In appearance at least, Mayburt was all that Bender and Moscow had described, a gravely handsome man, erect and alert.

"It appears to be a reasonable request, Captain Adams. Unless Major Smith has convincing reasons for desiring the witnesses to be present, the court will grant it."

Colonel Mayburt nodded at Smith, who rose and said, "May the court please, it would seem to me, sir, that my witnesses have every right to be present. They should certainly be kept aware of the progress of testimony."

Adams noticed that Coombs was whispering furiously to Wells, who shook his head. Coombs looked less than his twenty-two years. As assistant to Smith, he was already beginning to writhe with impatience, a small, boyish figure who had not yet learned to exercise patience toward insensitivity or stupidity.

"Witnesses have no *right* to be present, Major Smith. Their presence can only be at the court's dispensation," Thompson said. "What is your feeling, Colonel Mayburt?"

"I would be inclined for the court to exclude witnesses. Captain Adams has been more than reasonable in his waiver of challenges, and this is his first request."

129

"The court agrees to your request, Captain Adams," Colonel Thompson said. "The military police will escort the witnesses to the witness room. Captain O'Hara?" addressing the MP officer who stood behind the guests. "Will you see to it that the witnesses are not disturbed and that their comfort is provided for?"

Adams sat down and Bender whispered to him, "Oh, fine, sir. I am beginning to see what you mean."

"Just look at Morty Coombs," Moscow said.

Coombs was trying to talk to Smith, who shook his head impatiently.

☆ Monday 10.30 A. M.

Sergeant Albert Johnson was the first witness for the prosecution. Before the court convened, he had mentioned to Adams that it was an unexpected treat to get away from Bachree outside of his regular leave. He said that the nice thing about Bachree was that wherever else you found yourself, it was an improvement.

At half-past ten, Major Smith had finished his examination of Johnson, who was an excellent witness. He had good recall and a precise manner of expressing detail. He had told the story of the murder, presenting the same facts that Major Kensington had given to Adams. He did not color them, nor did any sense of self-importance lead him to dramatize the facts out of proportion. He was one of those dry, self-contained Englishmen who seem to be utterly unshakable.

Major Smith appeared to be pleased with both himself and his witness as he sat down. Colonel Thompson turned to Barney Adams and asked whether he would cross-examine.

"If it please the court?" Adams replied, rising and going around his end of the triple table. He passed behind Winston, who continued to sit in silence and indifference; and confronting Johnson, he realized that this was the first time, after so many years of study and preparation, that he was actually facing a witness in a military courtroom.

"You may proceed," Thompson directed.

"Sergeant Johnson," Adams said, "have you had any combat experience?"

"Yes, sir. Against the Japs in Burma, the defense of Rangoon and then the retreat."

"Were you a rifleman, machine gunner, mortar?"

"Rifleman, sir."

"What is your experience with side arms?"

"I have used them, sir. My lieutenant was killed, and we had to leave his body. I took his revolver and ammunition, and used it until the ammunition was gone."

"And then? What did you do with it?"

"I threw it into a supply lorry, sir."

"You made no attempt to replenish the ammunition?"

Both Wells and Coombs had scribbled notes to Major Smith, who rose at this point and entered an objection.

"If the court please," Smith said indignantly, "this is cross-examination. I can't conceivably see what this line of questioning has to do with the direct examination."

Thompson looked questioningly at Colonel Mayburt, who

131

said, "Captain Adams, do you intend a connection between this line of questioning and the direct examination?"

"I do, sir," Adams answered. "Also, if the court please, I have not called Sergeant Johnson as my witness. If I am allowed a certain amount of latitude—toward a connection, of course—I will not have to call him and can thereby save the court considerable time."

As he spoke, Colonel Mayburt wrote on a pad, which he passed to Thompson. Thompson read it, glanced at Mayburt, swallowed and said to Major Smith: "The court is fully aware of the laws of evidence, Major. It is commendable to object to a line of questioning that may appear to be improper—but perhaps the objection should be withheld until the direction is fully apparent. In that manner, we will expedite the progress of this trial." And then to Adams, "Please proceed, Captain—and to the point."

"Shall I repeat the question?" Adams asked Johnson.

"No, sir, I remember it. I made no attempt to replenish my ammunition."

"Why?"

"Because I consider a pistol or a revolver an inferior weapon. Accuracy beyond a few dozen feet is almost impossible. It cannot be properly aimed except under the best circumstances, and any attempt at rapid fire renders it worthless except as a source of noise."

His description of side arms brought smiles throughout the room. Adams saw Bender nudge Moscow and whisper to him.

"What is your own weapon at Bachree?" Adams asked.

"American carbine, sir."

"Oh? Not a British weapon?"

"We have a mixed complement at Bachree, sir. Our weapons are American issue. The carbine is a fine weapon."

132

"Now, Sergeant—I am fully aware that under stress, and not fully awake, a man cannot properly count shots. So I am prepared to accept your statement that you did not know whether Lieutenant Winston's pistol was empty. But you were aware that he was armed only with a pistol?"

"Yes, sir, I was."

"Could he have obtained a rifle or a carbine?"

"No, sir, he could not. All weapons except his own pistol were kept in the barracks. Once he left the barracks, he could not obtain a rifle at Bachree."

"Yet you testified, Sergeant Johnson, that after you saw Lieutenant Winston kill Sergeant Quinn, you watched him back out of the barracks door. He held his gun on you. Is that correct?" .

"Yes, sir."

"You also testified that your next action was to send someone to phone Major Kensington. Then you ordered the men in the barracks to get dressed. Not until they were fully dressed, did you allow the search for Lieutenant Winston to proceed?"

"That is correct, sir."

"How much time had elapsed by then?"

"I can't say for certain, sir. At least fifteen minutes."

"In other words, you deliberately allowed fifteen minutes to elapse before going after a murderer. Was it because of his pistol, Sergeant? You have already given your opinion of the pistol as a weapon. Was it because of that?"

"No, sir—" For the first time, Johnson hesitated momentarily before replying. "No, sir," he repeated, "not because of the pistol."

"Yet you testified that you were uncertain of whether or not he was armed with a loaded weapon?"

133

"Yes, sir, I did. But I was not asked why I did not go after Lieutenant Winston immediately."

Major Smith rose to anticipate the next question with an objection, but Adams put it aside unspoken and, instead of inquiring why Johnson had not done so, asked, "When you did go after Lieutenant Winston, how many men did you take with you?"

"All of them, sir, except for one man I sent to wait for Major Kensington at the road junction. We have a very small complement at Bachree, a dozen men with myself."

"And did you issue arms to all the men?"

Again Sergeant Johnson hesitated. Then, his former briskness and alertness gone, he slowly replied, "No, sir, I did not."

"With an armed murderer loose on the installation, you did not order a general issue of arms?"

"No, sir. I did not."

"Did you issue any arms?"

"Yes, sir. Corporal Goldman and I took our carbines."

"Please identify Corporal Goldman?"

"United States Army, Quartermaster, sir. After Lieutenant Winston's action and Sergeant Quinn's death, he was the ranking non-commissioned officer after myself.

"Sergeant Johnson, will you please tell the court why you issued only two carbines."

Both Coombs and Wells had been passing notes to Major Smith, who now rose and offered his objection.

"On what grounds, sir?" Colonel Thompson asked.

"May it please the court, this is not proper cross-examination. Sergeant Johnson did not testify on these matters."

Thompson looked at Mayburt, who said, "It would appear to me, Major Smith, that the connection is obvious. You took testimony on all the incidents of that night. The cross-examination would hardly be worth while if it did not elicit information absent in the direct examination. It is true that we follow federal court procedure to a large extent. But since this is not trial by civilian jury, we welcome the introduction of factual matter—so long as the general laws of evidence are observed."

He said this patiently and not unkindly, yet Major Smith recognized the blow and seated himself morosely.

Bender whispered to Moscow, "Morty Coombs must have guessed what's coming, but so help me, Thompson doesn't know. Look at him beaming on the captain."

Adams caught Moscow's eye and stopped the whispering. "You will answer the question, Sergeant," Thompson said.

"I issued only two carbines," Johnson stated slowly, "because I was afraid that men who had just seen a murder done might not hesitate to kill the murderer."

"You had also seen the murder done, as you testified, Sergeant Johnson. Did you have no desire to kill the murderer?"

"I did not."

"Out of solicitude for Lieutenant Winston."

"No, sir."

"Did you like Lieutenant Winston?"

"I did not like him."

"Yet, knowing he was armed with a pistol and knowing he was a murderer, you took pains to protect him?"

"Yes, sir—I suppose you could look at it that way."

"How did you look at it, Sergeant? Differently?"

"Yes, sir."

"Then please tell the court how you looked at it, Sergeant. Please explain your reasons for delay and for arming only two men."

Major Smith rose with more confidence now. "May it please the court, I must object to this line of questioning. Sergeant Johnson is not on trial for negligence. If such an inquiry is to be made, it is a matter for the British Command."

"The court will have to sustain this objection, Captain Adams," Thompson said. "Unless you can show that this is vital to the matter at hand."

"I withdraw that question."

"Strike it from the record, Sergeant Debbs," Mayburt said to the court reporter.

"When you began the search for Lieutenant Winston, it was your intention to take him alive—was it not, Sergeant?"

"It was."

"Why did you desire to take him alive?"

Sergeant Johnson hesitated, then blurted out, "Because Lieutenant Winston was insane! And I did not want the blood of an insane man on my hands!"

All three men of the prosecution rose to the objection. Winston himself raised his bent head and looked dully at Johnson. Wells and Coombs sank back to their seats. General Kempton, staring coolly and deliberately, attempted to catch Adams' glance; but Barney Adams watched the court, his face placid, his blue eyes mildly questioning.

Angry and frustrated, Major Smith denied Sergeant Johnson's competence. "I move that the question and answer be stricken."

Colonel Thompson made no reply to this. Colonel Mayburt passed him a note. Still Colonel Thompson did not react. Then he leaned across to Mayburt, and they talked in whispers for about a minute. Finally, Colonel Thompson nodded and then relaxed in his chair.

Colonel Mayburt said: "Your objection to the competence

of Sergeant Johnson's opinion, Major Smith, can only be sustained if he were to offer it as a diagnosis, which he is obviously not qualified to make. However, he is giving his reason for failing to take an action. This testimony is proper to cross-examination, and I cannot sustain an objection unless he offers the same opinion as a pretense at diagnosis."

Mayburt then turned to Adams and said, "You understand the position of the court, Captain Adams. You can elicit testimony from Sergeant Johnson on the facts of the night in question. You cannot probe into the reasons upon which Sergeant Johnson bases his answer."

"May it please the court," Adams said, "under these circumstances, I will reserve the right to recall this witness as a witness for the defense."

"That is your privilege, sir. I am sure you recognize that since Sergeant Johnson is a member of the British Armed Forces, he can appear only with the consent of his superior officers."

"Yes, sir. I do recognize that fact."

Thompson now said, a faint, muted note of anger in his voice, "Do you have any other questions, Captain Adams?"

"No, sir, I do not."

Wells and Coombs were whispering with Smith when Colonel Thompson turned to them. "Major Smith?"

Smith spread his hands to halt the conference, wearily nodding his submission. He rose to his feet.

"You may have the witness for redirect examination."

"There are no further questions, sir."

Colonel Thompson nodded and said to Johnson, "You will stand down, Sergeant. You are to hold yourself in waiting at the witness room, unless otherwise instructed."

He pursed his lips and looked at his watch. "Court will adjourn until one o'clock."

☆ *Monday 12.10 A. M.*

Lieutenant Bender had recommended the Chin Lee Soong, a Chinese restaurant, as a quiet place where they could eat lunch and talk. Corporal Baxter dropped them off there, and then took the jeep to the hospital to pick up Lieutenant Sorenson.

Under Bender's guidance, they had ordered a casserole of chicken cooked with pineapple and water chestnuts. Moscow and Adams only played with their food; Bender ate with the appetite of a man who has not seen food for days. To Adams, it did not taste like any chicken he had ever encountered, though the food was delicious, and he asked Bender what kind of chicken it was.

"Oh, it's not chicken, sir, it's pork."

"Then why do they call it chicken?"

"The Moslems, sir. They don't want to offend any Moslems."

"I should think the Moslems would be more offended by being tricked."

"No, sir, they're not tricked at all. No Moslem ever eats in a Chinese restaurant."

"I wouldn't press it, Captain," Moscow said. "Just let Harvey eat."

"Yes—I suppose so."

"Please, sir," Moscow said, "I can't get it out of my mind. When you began your line of questioning, you knew just where you were going. But how could you have known that Johnson would come right out and call Winston insane?"

"I didn't know."

"But you must have had some inkling—"

"There had to be some reason for the delay. I've seen the type of British soldier Johnson is. A pistol wouldn't stop him. But the implication of cowardice was more than he could bear."

"Do you think they'll let him testify for us, sir?" Bender asked.

"I wouldn't call him," Adams said. "There's nothing he could add to his testimony that we need."

"This morning," Moscow said thoughtfully, "I wouldn't have given a dollar to win twenty that there was any chance for an acquittal."

"And now, Lieutenant?"

"I'll be honest with you, Captain Adams. Now I'm afraid. It's like stopping a tank with your bare hands. Even if you stop it, it's got to roll over you. Up until now—well, I won't speak for Harvey, but for me it was like a game. They held all the cards. God, I said to myself, what a thing to pull this off—what a ramrod to shove up the ass of that snot-nose Morty Jacobs. But I didn't believe it."

Adams looked at Bender, who went on eating silently and deliberately. Then Baxter came into the restaurant, with Kate Sorenson.

The three men rose, and Adams introduced the two lieu-

139

tenants. Then he said to Baxter, "Sit down at a table over there, Corporal, and have some lunch. We'll leave here at exactly ten minutes to one. You're my guest this time."

"Look, Captain, you don't have to buy me lunch."

"Only when I choose the restaurant, Baxter. Go on, now—we have little enough time."

Baxter sat down at a table across the room and ordered lunch. Lieutenant Bender heaped a plateful of food for Kate Sorenson, who was watching Adams strangely and newly, as if she had not seen him before. He himself was thinking that he had not seen her face by daylight. He could not really remember the woman in Major Kaufman's office; this was another person.

"I'm very glad to see you, Barney. How did it go this morning?"

"As well as I could have expected."

Lieutenant Bender opened his mouth, began to say something, and then swallowed his words. Moscow was watching Sorenson with undisguised approval.

"You got my note, of course?" Sorenson said.

"Yes. But you don't have to do this, Kate. As a matter of fact, I don't want you to."

"You didn't feel that way about Max Kaufman."

Groping for his words, Adams said to her, "Until now, Kate, it was different. Lieutenant Moscow here said that it was like a game for him. Maybe it was like a game for me, too. Today, I'm too old to play games any more. I'm going to win this case because it must be won. I can't spell that out yet, because I'm still grappling with it in my own mind, but I know it. And if it is won, people will be hurt."

"I've been hurt before," she said.

"Will it do any good to argue with you?"

"No, it won't."

"Very well. Show me the letter."

Sorenson took a folded piece of paper out of her purse and handed it to Adams. He read it slowly and thoughtfully, while his two assistants watched him with unconcealed curiosity. Then he refolded the letter and handed it back to the nurse.

"I won't begin my own case until tomorrow," he said. "You will have to be at the Judge Advocate General's all day—unless I begin early. Corporal Baxter will pick you up along with Major Kaufman at about nine in the morning. Is that all right?"

She nodded. Adams turned to his assistants. "Which one of you knows something about the local university?"

"It's not much of a university, sir," Moscow replied. "Not in our terms. Their plant is falling in, and the teachers are even poorer than the pupils. I guess Harvey knows the place better than I do."

"I gave a lecture there on Anglo-Saxon common law last month," Bender admitted. "It wasn't much of a lecture, sir, but I was dating a girl from the faculty and I couldn't very well refuse when she asked me."

"Bender, I want a handwriting expert," Adams said. "I can't think of any other place where I might get one. What are the chances of finding one there?"

"Heaven only knows, sir. I can't think of any reason why they should have one."

"Suppose you find out. If you can't find one at the university, put out feelers wherever you can, the local police, the enlisted men—wherever you can. Come to think of it, the local police must know of a handwriting expert. When you find him, try to persuade him to be a witness tomorrow. His

141

expenses will be paid, and I'll stand for any extra loss he may feel he must take."

"Suppose he won't respond to persuasion?"

"Don't threaten any subpoena unless you have to."

"Shall I tell him what case it is?"

"You'll have to—of course. But the fewer details you offer, the better."

Sorenson said, "If other things fail, try the offices of the *Daily Announcer*. Ask for a reporter called Sundar Jatee. He thinks well of the captain, and he's not too afraid."

"Good idea," Adams agreed. "Now, I want you to remain here with Lieutenant Sorenson until Baxter returns. You can have the jeep and Baxter until court adjourns."

Baxter was at the table now, glancing at his watch. Adams looked at Sorenson searchingly. "Thank you, Kate," he said.

☆ Monday 1.00 P.M.

When the court convened for its afternoon session, Major Smith put Corporal Robert Goldman on the stand. Corporal Goldman was a stolid young man with sandy hair, pale blue eyes, and a painstakingly deliberate manner of answering questions. Adams was not surprised to hear that Goldman had not lost his head or become unduly disturbed on the night in question; the corporal gave the impression that nothing on earth could disturb him and that midnight murders were not uncommon in his life.

His story was essentially the same as Sergeant Johnson's, except that he had awakened a few moments later, and reached the door to the separate room where Johnson and Quinn slept just as Winston opened fire.

When Goldman had finished testifying, Colonel Thompson nodded at Adams and said, "You may cross-examine, Captain Adams."

"I have no questions," Adams replied. Both Smith and Thompson were startled; and Adams wondered whether he had seen just a trace of a smile on Colonel Mayburt's face. He couldn't be sure.

Moscow passed him a note, which said, "I like that. It was damn good timing."

"Now, I think, they are beginning to doubt just a little," Adams whispered to him. He saw Winston sitting motionless, hands clasped in his lap.

Moscow began to write as Major Smith called Colonel Archer Burton to the stand. The note Moscow handed to Adams now read: "Winston spoke to me on the way in. He said, God will emerge and strike today. He said that his side is inflamed with a red spot where God is trying to come out. That is why he is sitting so still. To help God. Is this a line?"

Adams wrote, "No," and passed the note back.

Colonel Burton was sworn in. He gave his name and his rank. He stated that he was commanding officer at the General Hospital, and then he answered a number of questions concerning the table of organization at the hospital.

"On the morning that Lieutenant Winston was admitted to the hospital—were you there, Colonel Burton?"

"I was at the hospital. I believe that at the precise time

143

Lieutenant Winston was admitted, I was in my office, discussing our surgical service with Colonel Hale, our chief of surgery."

"Were you notified of his admittance, Colonel?"

"Not until four hours later. It was not until then that I heard about the murder. Headquarters called me. Captain Greene, my assistant, was with me. He told me that this man, Lieutenant Winston, had been admitted to the hospital that morning."

"Was it ordinary procedure, Colonel, to admit patients without notifying you?"

"Yes, ordinary procedure. But this was not an ordinary patient. Major Kaufman, the physician who admitted him, should have notified me immediately."

"But he did not?"

"No, sir, he did not."

Smith nodded and said, "Would you tell us what you did then, sir?"

"I phoned Major Kaufman immediately and asked him on what basis Winston had been admitted—"

"Excuse me, Colonel Burton," Smith interrupted, "but in order that our record may show it, will you identify Major Kaufman more specifically. Name in full, rank, and position."

"Major Max Kaufman, U.S. Army Medical Corps, General Hospital, officer chief of NP Ward."

"What do the initials N. P. stand for, Colonel Burton?"

"Neuro-Psychopathic."

"Thank you. Now I believe you said that you phoned Major Kaufman and asked him why he admitted Lieutenant Winston."

"I did. He said that Winston was sick, and that was why he had admitted him. I asked him how he was sick. He replied

144

that Lieutenant Winston was in a profound confusional and depressed state." Colonel Burton smiled. "I think I have his words."

During this, Mayburt had passed a note to Thompson, who nodded. Mayburt said, "The court will interrupt you at this point, Major Smith."

"May it please the court," Smith acquiesced.

Adams noticed that Moscow had scribbled the word *hearsay* several times on his pad, but he made no move to pass it.

Mayburt turned to Adams and said, "Would you stand, Captain Adams."

Adams rose, and Mayburt continued, "Are you aware, Captain, that the evidence just taken is hearsay evidence, and therefore inadmissible?"

"May it please the court, I was aware that this is hearsay evidence."

"Will you tell the court why you did not offer an objection?"

"I rested upon an exception."

Only Winston was not listening with intentness. Moscow stared at Adams curiously, frowning in spite of himself. Coombs was scribbling furiously. General Kempton's face wore a placid expression that Barney Adams was beginning to know and understand; his eyes were narrow, lazy slits.

Colonel Thompson's round, pink-cheeked face tightened, and directing one pudgy finger at Adams, he said: "The court desires you to understand, Captain Adams, that this case is not to be taken lightly. Not only is it a capital case, but under the present conditions of total war, its importance transcends its circumstances. The court will spare no effort to present a record that is free from error—even the error of insolence."

145

"May the court please," Adams replied earnestly, "I meant no insolence. If any implication of insolence could be read into my words or attitude, I apologize."

Mayburt had passed another note to Thompson. Then they put their heads together. The pink of Thompson's cheeks grew deeper. Major Hennessy passed a note down the table —the first non-presiding member of the court-martial to take any action. Thompson and Mayburt read it together. Thompson then nodded, a quick little nod. His lips were tight.

Mayburt said, "Sergeant Debbs, it is the desire of the president that both his statement and Captain Adams' apology should be stricken from the record." Then, to Adams, as if nothing at all had transpired, "Why do you rest upon an exception, Captain Adams?"

"May it please the court, there is precedent for defense counsel's willingness to accept hearsay evidence so taken. In the interest of the facts, sir, such exception has been established."

"I have no knowledge of such exception ever being offered by the counsel not conducting the examination. It would be understandable for Major Smith to cite this exception. But why do you cite it, Captain?"

"Because, sir, I believe it to be in the public interest."

"Have you any precedent in military trial, Captain Adams?"

"In Corporal Fredericks versus the United States Army, France, 1918, and in Captain Lewis versus the United States Army, Arizona, 1906. There are other cases which I cannot immediately call to mind. If the court so desires, I may be able to find them and cite them."

"It will not be necessary," Colonel Mayburt replied, a trace of a smile on his face. "The court will permit hearsay evidence to be taken, but limited to the conversation with Major Kauf-

146

man. At the same time, Captain Adams, the court will permit no cross-examination on the hearsay evidence, for that would constitute an entrapment which we cannot permit."

"May it please the court, I have no intention of entrapment of any kind. I only desire that full and truthful evidence be taken."

"We all desire that, Captain Adams." And to Smith, "Proceed with your witness, Major Smith."

"May it please the court," Smith said, "I did not deliberately attempt to extract hearsay evidence. I will be more aware of it from here on."

"The court understands this, Major."

"May I thank the court." Smith returned to his witness, and asked Burton, "Did you conduct a personal examination of the defendant, Lieutenant Winston, Colonel?"

"I did."

"And when was that?"

"Firstly, the day after he was brought into the hospital. Then, again, two days later."

"In other words, you examined him twice."

"I did."

"And what were the results of your examination?"

"On the first occasion his pulse was rather rapid. He was suffering from a general fatigue brought on by lack of food and sleep. On the second occasion his pulse was normal and the fatigue had decreased."

"Would you say he was in good health on the occasion of the second examination?"

"Not good health in the abstract. But I suspect his health was as good as it has been for the past year. Lieutenant Winston went through a siege of ulcers some five years ago. He also suffers from a nervous stomach. I would say that for him, on the occasion of my second examination, his health was quite normal."

"Did he appear to be excited?"

"Not at all."

Smith had turned back to his table, where Coombs passed him a note. He read it, then asked Burton, "Did he appear depressed—that is, Lieutenant Winston?"

"No more than one would expect, considering the circumstances."

"Then on the basis of your two examinations, Colonel Burton, did you find any indication that Lieutenant Winston was—well—let us say, mentally sick? I believe that is the proper term—mentally sick."

"I did not."

"Did you find anything that would lead you to believe— that is, I mean to conclude—that Lieutenant Winston was insane?"

"I did not."

"Do you believe that such a condition could be present without your being aware of it?"

"No, sir, I do not. I do not wish to plead my competence. I think my position and rank indicate competence."

"Unquestionably, Colonel Burton. I did not intend to question your competence. Now, having found that Lieutenant Winston was sound of body and mind, what did you do?"

"Knowing that he was a murderer and having been advised by Theater Headquarters that he should stand trial as soon as possible, I suggested to Major Kaufman that he should be immediately discharged."

"And was he so discharged, Colonel Burton?"

"He was not."

"Will you tell the court the reasons why? Not any conversations that might have taken place between you and Major Kaufman, but the reason itself."

"Major Kaufman refused to sign his discharge papers."

"Did he give a reason why he refused?"

"Yes." Colonel Burton nodded, smiling slightly, his air one of forgive and forget. "His reason was that Lieutenant Winston was insane."

With this, almost all eyes in the room turned, with scarcely any conscious volition, upon Winston. But he appeared not to have heard. His face tilted up, smiling slightly, he sat rigid and unmoving.

Colonel Burton and Major Smith were among the exceptions. Neither of them looked at Winston. Major Smith phrased another question.

"Did he have the power to prevent such discharge? Major Kaufman, I mean."

"Not technically, no. As commanding officer of the hospital, I could have ordered such a discharge. But it is not the procedure we follow. A patient should properly be discharged from the section of the hospital he is treated in—and by the chief of that section."

"What did you do then, Colonel Burton?"

"I reported this to Headquarters. I was instructed by General Kempton to convene a lunacy commission and examine Lieutenant Winston."

"Did you or General Kempton suggest the lunacy commission?"

"I did."

"May I ask why, Colonel?"

"So that the question of Winston's sanity would be settled once and for all and beyond doubt."

Colonel Thompson now leaned across the table and said,

149

"The court realizes that giving testimony is a difficult affair, Colonel Burton. Nevertheless, I must ask you to address the defendant by his rank. Until the verdict of this court is rendered, he holds that rank in the United States Army."

Colonel Burton apologized gracefully, and then Major Smith asked him to explain to the court just what a lunacy commission was.

"A special commission called by the commanding officer above the rank of divisional commander to pass upon questions of sanity and insanity."

"And who was appointed to this commission?"

"Colonel Joseph Hale and Major Richard Frank, both of them physicians on the hospital staff, and myself."

"Had the commission a head?"

"I was the chief officer of the commission."

"Did this lunacy commission examine Lieutenant Winston?"

"It did."

"On what date?"

"The sixth day after he had been admitted to the hospital."

"Was this a full and thorough examination?"

"It was."

"And what were the findings of the lunacy commission, Colonel Burton?"

"The commission found Lieutenant Winston to be sane, both fit and responsible to stand trial."

"What action did you take in Lieutenant Winston's case then, Colonel?"

"I signed the order for his discharge. The following morning he was picked up at the hospital by the military police and taken to the Provost."

150

"Thank you, Colonel Burton. That will be all."

With satisfaction, Major Smith turned to Adams and said, "Your witness, Captain Adams."

☆ *Monday 2.12 P.M.*

As Barney Adams listened to Colonel Burton's testimony, he began to realize the full implication of what he proposed to do. Realizing it, he had to confront himself with his reasons; and strangely enough, for the first time, the whole structure and meaning of the Winston affair came into a sort of focus. At first this focus was blurred and uncertain; over the next twenty-four hours it clarified itself and became precise.

While Burton was testifying, Adams passed a note to Moscow—"You are free to disassociate yourself, if you wish to. I think I understand your position."

The reply read, "I don't think you do. I'm staying. So is Harvey, so you don't have to ask him. We talked about it."

Adams nodded. He had come to like Bender and Moscow a good deal.

At twelve minutes after two, he rose for the cross-examination and said to Colonel Burton, "Colonel, in your testimony you said that four hours passed after Lieutenant Winston was admitted to the hospital—before you heard about it. Is that so?"

"That is right."

"Did you intend to imply that Major Kaufman deliberately kept the information from you?"

"I have no idea what Major Kaufman intended. I intended to imply nothing except that four hours had passed."

"Colonel Burton, do you know whether Major Kaufman deliberately withheld the information?"

"Major Kaufman has not been particularly co-operative. There is no reason for me to think that he might not have withheld the information."

"I am not asking for your reasons to think this or that, Colonel. I am asking whether you know something. Please answer yes or no."

"I do not know for certain."

"Thank you, sir. Now, can you tell the court how Captain Greene, your assistant, came to have the information before you did?"

"I am afraid you will have to ask Captain Greene that. I am a busy man, Captain Adams, commanding a large hospital."

"Again, sir," Adams said quietly, "I must ask you to answer my question."

Major Smith then rose and asked the court whether Captain Adams could badger a witness in this fashion.

Thompson turned to Mayburt uncertainly, and Mayburt said: "This is not badgering, Major Smith. Captain Adams is addressing the witness with propriety and within the framework of proper cross-examination. This court is not interested in concealment. I must ask you to be a little more certain of your grounds before you interrupt counsel again."

And to Burton, he said, "Colonel Burton, you will answer the questions as put."

152

"No, I do not know. I may have known at the time—if so, it has passed out of my mind as a matter of no importance."

"Perhaps we should suspend judgment on whether or not this is important, Colonel Burton. Now I ask you, is it regular procedure at the hospital for the physician in charge of a particular patient to prepare a report on that patient's condition and progress?"

Colonel Burton tightened his lips and stared straight before him. His cheeks lost color and he blinked rapidly. The seconds passed and he made no reply.

"Please answer my question, sir," Adams said patiently.

Still Colonel Burton sat in silence. The silence pervaded the room. It hung as heavy as molasses.

Suddenly Major Cummings spoke up, his voice cutting the silence like a knife, "With your permission, Colonel Thompson, may I ask whether there is any reason why Colonel Burton should not answer that question?"

"Approach the bench, sir," Thompson said to Adams. Thompson's voice was hoarse and thick. Adams walked up to where Thompson and Mayburt were sitting. Mayburt was listening and watching with puzzled curiosity and some annoyance as well.

"Captain Adams," Thompson whispered, "do you intend to go on with this line of questioning?"

"Yes, sir. I do."

"Are you certain?"

Mayburt broke into the whispered conversation, "I am sorry to have to interfere, Colonel Thompson, but I think this is highly improper."

"I have said nothing that is improper."

"This whole approach is improper," Mayburt whispered angrily. "There is no conceivable reason within my knowledge of law why Burton should not have been directed to answer that question. It was a proper question, and it is not for the court to challenge Captain Adam's approach."

"I hardly think this should be discussed here and now."

"With all due respect, sir," Mayburt said, still whispering, "I think you invited discussion. I would suggest a brief recess."

"You may return to your place, Captain Adams," Thompson said; and then, when Adams had stepped away, he rapped with his gavel and announced, "The court will recess until three o'clock."

☆ Monday 2.30 P.M.

As they left the court, General Kempton ranged himself alongside of Barney Adams and said, "Suppose we have a word or two, Barney."

"Certainly, sir."

"Unless you need this time?"

"I didn't anticipate the recess, sir, so my time is at your disposal."

General Kempton led the way to Colonel Thompson's office at the end of the hallway opposite the courtroom. He closed the door behind them, took a cigarette for himself and then offered one to Adams.

154

"Smoke?"

"Thank you, sir."

"Do you ever swear, Barney?"

"Sir?"

"Lose your temper—let go? Would you derive no satisfaction from just roaring out that this is a shit-ass, lousy, mother-friggen, second-rate sonofabitch world?"

"I suppose I might under certain circumstances," Adams replied, without any particular interest or enthusiasm.

"Your generation puzzles me." The general shook his head. "If I could indulge the idiocy that passes for thought in some of my associates, I might infer that we were a generation of men and you are a generation of patsys. That would be shoddy reasoning, wouldn't it, Barney?"

"Possibly, sir. Most generalizations tend to fall flat."

"I'm a deceitful old bastard," the general said thoughtfully, pacing back and forth from window to door and door to window, "but there are occasions when I say what is on my mind. There are times when I let go and let it pour out. But I have a notion that no one ever looks past your face, Barney. That fine, innocent, open and stupid American face that tells the whole world that we're a nation of idiot patsys, of fourth-generation backwoods boobs, of Boy Scouts dressed in dollar bills. Yes, I said to myself—there's the boy for me, Barney Adams, my old pal's son—there's the boy to rally round the flag—"

He stopped pacing, ground out his cigarette on Colonel Thompson's polished floor, and flung one arm at Adams: "Just who in hell are you defending, sir? Tell me that! You're not defending Winston! Or are you?"

Within himself, what Adams felt was not new. He had had this feeling before, the surflike pounding of his heart,

155

the trembling of every limb, the beginning of terrible rage that only began and never culminated, the quivering of his fingers so that he clenched his hands to control them. This was the feeling of danger to himself by himself, and he was more afraid of it than he was of anything else. So he told himself: This is a general and you are a soldier, and a long, long time ago, it was decided that you would be a soldier, and you don't whimper or cry—and above all you do not say things that you will regret.

All General Kempton saw was a man standing before him, a tall, good-looking, redheaded man who was not perturbed or upset by anything the general had said.

"Are you?" General Kempton repeated.

"No, I am not defending Charles Winston," Adams answered softly.

"Then who the devil are you defending?"

"Myself."

"What?"

Adams shook his head. "I can't put it any better."

Kempton resumed his pacing, his head bent. "God damn it, Barney," he said, "look at it my way."

"I do, sir. But I don't see it your way."

"I only ask you to look—to listen—to open that friggen Boy Scout mind of yours to a world of reality! Don't you think I know what they're saying—here, yes and in Washington and London too. They're saying—Don't worry. Kempton has it under control. Old Kempton is a hell of an able man, and that lousy, rotten Winston affair will finish up just the way Kempton wants it to. Kempton will fix it, they're saying, and the court will bring in the verdict Kempton wants. It's already decided. Do you think it's already decided, Barney?"

"No, sir, I do not."

"Do you think I can fix a trial like this?"

"No, sir, I don't think you can."

"Look what in hell I'm saddled with—that horse's ass Thompson for a Judge Advocate General—talking me into making him president of the court, and myself being fool enough to do it and invite prejudice! And that mother's mistake of a Major Smith for a trial counsel! Look at them! Look at the lot of them!"

"They're your men, General Kempton," Adams answered, unable now to keep the bitterness from his voice.

"Oh? And I suppose Archer Burton is my man too?"

"I don't know, sir."

"In a few minutes we go back in there. Archer Burton is standing naked, his thin little mind shivering with fear. What are you going to do, Barney—destroy him?"

"Yes."

"Why? Just tell me why?"

"Because," Adams said deliberately, "he is a liar, a cheat and a coward. Because he's covered himself with dirt and it rubs off everywhere, and because I am dirty with the same dirt—and I can't live with it. Maybe this way I can make myself a little cleaner."

"What in hell are you talking about?"

"It's ten minutes to three, sir."

"Wait a minute, Barney," the general said, halting his pacing, "and just don't go off half-cocked." His voice became softer, persuasive. "We're not strangers. You're the son of one of my best friends. We share something, an old and glorious tradition—as phony as that may sound. You must have understood that. What else led you to resign a commission in the Advocate's and go off and enlist in the infantry? You've made it the hard way—those bars on your shoulders,

157

you've won them in the field. No one gave them to you. When I say that anything is worth the price if it brings unity to this theater, then you know what I am talking about."

"I know."

"That's what I wanted to see—" the general began.

But Adams interrupted, "No, not what you wanted to see, sir! You don't buy unity by framing the hanging of a sick and insane man! You don't buy victory by rigging a murder trial! You buy destruction that way—you buy—"

"Barney!"

Adams stopped. His face was white, his hands clenched stiffly by his sides.

"All right, Captain Adams," the general said. "You have made yourself clear. You said destruction before. Go ahead and destroy yourself, Captain Adams."

☆ *Monday 3.00 P.M.*

Barney Adams returned to the courtroom through a crowd of pleading reporters, who knew that something of importance had happened—but as yet could find no indication of what that something was. However, before the day was to finish, the events of the afternoon would be public knowledge—at least in general outline. Adams had already come to realize that no court-martial is secret, whether or not the doors are closed.

The court came to order quickly and deliberately. Whatever had happened during the half-hour of recess had changed the court—and no one present now failed to sense the change. The change was in the faces of the court, the eyes of the officers, in the way they sat in their chairs, and in the way they watched and listened.

The change was also heard in the flat, tired tones of Colonel Thompson's voice as he said to Sergeant Debbs, "You will read the last question Captain Adams addressed to Colonel Burton!"

"Perhaps we should suspend judgment on whether or not this is important, Colonel Burton," Sergeant Debbs read from his notes. "Now I ask you, is it regular procedure at the hospital for the physician in charge of a particular patient to prepare a report on that patient's condition and progress?"

"You will answer that question, sir," Colonel Thompson said to Burton.

"Yes, that is our procedure," Colonel Burton said.

"And in the case of the defendant, Lieutenant Charles Winston—was such a report prepared?" Adams asked.

"Well—well, sir, I said that it was procedure. It is."

"That is not what I asked you, Colonel. I asked you whether in the case of Lieutenant Charles Winston such a report was prepared?"

"Probably so."

Adams voice hardened as he said, "No, Colonel, you are under oath. If you know the answer to my question, please be good enough to offer it to the court."

"I answered your question."

Colonel Mayburt's voice cut in. "No, sir—you did not answer the question. Do you understand, sir, that you sit as a witness in a court of law? Answer yes or no!"

"Yes," Burton whispered.

Adams walked over to Moscow, who handed him a sheaf of paper, eleven sheets stapled together. He took this and gave it to Burton and demanded, "Is this that report to which you referred, sir?"

"I don't know."

"Then examine, it, Colonel. It is dated, Colonel. It is typed on the hospital stationery, is it not? It is marked—Lieutenant Charles Winston. It bears his serial number. It is titled *History and Prognosis*. And it is signed with Major Kaufman's signature. Is that not so, Colonel?"

"Yes, that appears to be the case."

"May it please the court," Adams said, "I would like this to be stamped for identification. And then, if the court so pleases, I would like it to be entered for evidence, to be marked Defense Exhibit A."

Thompson had withdrawn into a shell of anger and control; he sat by Mayburt with an invisible wall between them. He tried to display disdain in the slight nod of his head that turned the proceedings of law over to the Law Officer.

But Mayburt remained unruffled as he said, "Mark it for identification, Sergeant Simmons, and then bring it to the bench."

Adams handed it to Simmons, the clerk, who stamped and dated it and then brought it to Thompson. He only glanced at it before he passed it to Mayburt. Mayburt leafed through it, and then passed it on. It went to Kelly, McCabe, Cummings and Brown; and then down the table again to Winovich, Burnside, Hennessy and Clement. During this time a restless silence pervaded the courtroom; whispers edged it with sound. But Kempton and his guests did not whisper—they sat each

160

in his own tension, concern or interest. Little rivers of perspiration flowed down Burton's cheeks.

Only Charles Winston was indifferent. Winston, with his hatred and hope, waited for God; but from all that he displayed, what happened in the courtroom never entered the shell that enclosed him.

The report came back to Mayburt. "You may enter it as evidence, Captain Adams," he said.

Adams took the report and gave it to Burton again. "This is a carbon copy, Colonel Burton," he said. "Have you ever seen the original?"

"I haven't had a chance to read this. How do I know if I have seen the original?"

"Then examine it and refresh your memory, Colonel." Adams waited a few moments more while Burton looked through the report. Then Adams asked, "Colonel Burton, did you read a report prepared by Major Kaufman on the case of Lieutenant Winston?"

"Yes, I read a report."

"Does this appear to be a copy of that report?"

"It does," Burton answered reluctantly.

Adams took it from him and read from the first page. "From page one of Major Kaufman's report, I quote: 'After making arrangements for Lieutenant Winston to be placed in a room, under guard, I informed the office of the commanding officer of the admittance and the circumstances surrounding it. This was during the first half-hour after the patient's arrival. I spoke to Captain Greene, assistant to the commanding officer, and related the fact to him. I pressed him to inform the commanding officer immediately, and he said that he would.' I end the quote there.

"Now, Colonel Burton, in your testimony you stated with-

161

out any qualification that you were not informed for four hours. Either Captain Greene was guilty of gross negligence or you were not telling the truth. Which is it?"

"I may have forgotten that Captain Greene mentioned it earlier."

"Do you remember now, sir?"

"I seem to recollect something of the sort. I am a very busy man. Sometimes things do not impress themselves on me sufficiently."

"But you are sufficiently impressed with the fact that you are now under oath?"

Major Smith rose with an objection. His anger bursting forth at this point, he cried out, "May it please the court, Colonel Burton is not on trial. I object to this whole line of questioning!"

"He's absolutely right," Thompson whispered bitterly to Mayburt.

Mayburt said, "Sergeant Debbs, strike out Captain Adams' last remark. And hereafter, Captain Adams, confine your questions to the cross-examination." Then he turned to Major Smith. "The court must overrule your objection to the entire line of questioning. It is proper cross-examination. I suggest you refer to your notes of your own direct examination." He then nodded at Adams to continue.

Adams said to Burton, "You said, sir, that you personally examined the defendant on two occasions. Did you take his blood pressure?"

"I don't remember," Burton replied.

"Did you check his reflex reactions?"

"I am not sure—I don't think so."

"You said in your testimony, Colonel, that you did take his pulse. What was his pulse beat on each occasion?"

"I can't remember—do you know how many—"

"Please, Colonel, in your testimony you spoke of his pulse being rapid the first time and normal the second time. Can you recollect that and not the number of beats per minute?"

"I can. And if you were a physician, you would understand."

"Yes, I suppose so. Now you testified that in both of your examinations you found nothing to lead you to believe that Lieutenant Winston was mentally sick. Is that so?"

"Yes, sir."

"I read from Defense Exhibit A, page two, quote: 'Upon admittance, the patient was in a profound suicidal-depressive state, which worsened the following day, and therefore could not be left unguarded for a moment. His pulse was 130, his blood pressure dangerously high. He was only vaguely aware of what had transpired the night before at Bachree, and his speech was incoherent. Not until after the third day of treatment and sedation could he be questioned in a manner that would evoke coherent response.' End quote.

"Does this suggest mental illness, Colonel?"

"I spoke only of my own examination," Burton said, some of his confidence returning.

"And you found none of these symptoms in your examination?"

"I mentioned that his pulse was rapid."

"Only that, sir?"

"That is what I mentioned."

"Yes, sir. And then you testified that Major Kaufman had refused to sign the discharge papers for the defendant?"

"Yes—he refused."

Major Smith rose, and Adams said, "May it please the court, I have no intention of cross-examining in terms of the hearsay evidence." White with anger, Major Smith reseated himself.

Adams went on, "Did Major Kaufman submit his report to you before or after he refused to discharge Lieutenant Winston?"

"I believe it was before."

"Did you read the report?"

"I did."

"Did you read all of it, Colonel?"

"I read most of it."

"Yet you saw fit to reject it?"

"As I told you some days ago, Captain Adams, the report was not competent or scientific."

"And you came to this conclusion without even reading the entire report?"

"I am a medical man, sir. I can recognize incompetence."

"Did you tell Major Kaufman to prepare another report?"

"I did."

"Did you advise him to change his conclusions?"

"I advised him to restudy the case."

"Did you advise him to find Lieutenant Winston sane?"

"I advised him to restudy the case."

"I see. Now, Colonel Burton, you testified that General Kempton instructed you to convene a lunacy commission. Who selected the members of this commission?"

"I did, upon the recommendation of General Kempton."

"Do you mean that he asked you to choose the members? Or did he select them himself?"

"He asked me to choose the members."

"Yes, thank you, sir. Now *lunacy* is a legalistic term which today is no longer used in medical practice. Am I right, sir?"

"It could still be used in medical practice."

"But, Colonel, since Webster's International Dictionary, a

copy of which we have in this courtroom, defines psychiatry as the medical specialty which deals with mental disorders, would it not be proper and perhaps more modern, in sense, to refer to a lunacy commission as a psychiatric commission?"

"I suppose it could be so referred to."

"Thank you. Now in your General Hospital, sir, do you have a Department of Psychiatry?"

"We have the Neuro-Psychopathic Ward."

"How many beds are in this ward?"

"There are two buildings with two hundred beds."

Adams walked across to Moscow and accepted a slip of paper he held out.

Then, to Burton, "Would this be a proper description of the work of your NP Ward? I have taken this from the physicians in charge. Psychotic section—schizophrenic, acute mania, confusional states, paranoid states, depression. Neurotic section—psychosomatic, depression, traumatic neurosis, compulsion."

"Yes, if you wish to use fancy language."

"This is not language of my choosing or competence, sir. These are medical terms. I merely repeat them. Now, how many physicians work in the NP Ward?"

"Three."

"Would you name them, Colonel?"

"Major Kaufman, Captain Mayer and Captain Albertson."

"Are they all trained psychiatrists?"

"I don't know," Burton snapped.

"Are you seriously telling me, sir, that you do not know whether the three physicians who have the responsibility for your mental patients are trained psychiatrists or not?"

"Yes, I am."

"May I remind you that you are under oath, Colonel."

"I must object to this incredible procedure," Major Smith declared. "May the court please—this whole line of questioning and implication is improper and incompetent."

Colonel Thompson nodded and added, "Your constant reminders to Colonel Burton that he is under oath are offensive, Captain Adams. You are not examining a criminal, but an officer and a gentleman who accepts the role of a cooperative witness."

"May it please the court," Adams said, "I have attempted to avoid any error in proper cross-examination. If my remark was in poor taste, I apologize to the court. May I continue?"

"May I have a ruling on my objection, if the court so pleases?" Smith asked.

Mayburt, his face set and empty of expression, scribbled on his pad.

Thompson said angrily, "The objection is not in order. You are overruled, Major Smith."

"I ask you again, Colonel," Adams persisted, "are these three officers trained psychiatrists?"

"I don't know."

Again Adams took a paper from Moscow. "May it please the court, this is a précis of the medical and training records of the officers in question. May it be marked for identification and entered as evidence?"

As this was done, an almost palpable gloom settled over the court. The room was heavy with heat. It had darkened through the afternoon, and now, outside, it began to rain.

"May it please the court," Adams said, "I would request that the record show that the three officers in charge of the NP Ward at the General Hospital are trained and qualified psychiatrists."

"It is so ordered, Sergeant Debbs," Mayburt said bluntly.

"Colonel Burton," Adams said, his face bleak and tired, "you convened a lunacy commission, in other words a psychiatric commission, and made no attempt to place one of the three psychiatrists on your staff upon it. Is that not so?"

Colonel Burton tightened his lips.

A long moment went past, and then Colonel Mayburt leaned forward and said, "As the Law Officer of this court, Colonel Burton, I must instruct you that when you are under oath and a proper question is asked, you are to answer it. This court will decide when a question is improper. It is not for you to decide. This court is not influenced by rank or circumstances. There is no rank higher than a court of the United States Army. And unless you co-operate with this court, it will not hesitate to find you in contempt. May I say that I find your conduct disturbing, your answers confusing and perilously close to perjury." Mayburt's face was white with anger as he sat back.

"I will rephrase that question," Adams said. "Why did you not appoint a psychiatrist to the lunacy commission?"

"I did not think they were competent," Burton answered slowly.

"I see. Colonel Hale is a surgeon, is he not?"

"Yes, he is."

"And Major Frank is a dentist, is he not?"

"He is."

"But you decided that both these men were competent to sit upon a lunacy commission with a man's life at stake. Is that so, sir?"

"Yes."

"Did Colonel Hale or Major Frank conduct physical examinations of the defendant, Lieutenant Winston?"

"No, they did not."

"Was Major Kaufman's report given to them to read?"

"I don't know."

"I submit that you do know!" Adams cried. "Was the report given to them?"

"It was not."

"And yourself, sir, what were your reasons for appointing yourself head of the commission?"

"I believed I was competent. I am the commanding officer of a general hospital," Burton answered desperately.

"I see. Have you ever had any psychiatric training, Colonel Burton?"

"Not in a formal sense, no."

"Then in an informal sense, you have. Will you explain that, sir?"

"I have studied books on the subject."

"Will you tell the court the title and author of one or more of these books?"

"That was some time ago. I don't recollect the titles."

"I see. Now here again, sir, is Major Kaufman's report. On page three, I read, quote, 'All the symptoms of schizophrenic-paranoia were present in a marked manner, as follows—' I end quote.

"Do you know what those symptoms are, Colonel?"

"No, I don't. I know when a man is sane or insane. That's enough to know."

"Could you tell the court the meaning of schizophrenic-paranoia?"

Colonel Burton sat stolidly silent, but one arm was trembling now, from shoulder to hand.

"Colonel Burton," Adams said deliberately, "where were you employed before you enlisted in the army?" And when

Burton did not answer, Adams continued, "Was it in the Diamond-Square Truck Works in Detroit?"

"Yes."

"Were you employed as company physician?"

"Yes."

"And were you discharged because you diagnosed a heart attack as acute indigestion?"

"I was not discharged," Burton said, his voice a whimper now. "I resigned."

"I have no further questions," Adams told the court—without any note of triumph or joy.

☆ Monday 4.40 P.M.

Colonel Burton was the last witness for the prosecution. After he had left the witness chair, Major Smith announced that he was resting his case.

"If the court pleases," he said, "and with the reservation that if the defense chooses to make a closing statement I may reply to it, the United States Army is prepared to rest on the evidence that has been taken. In the light of this evidence, I feel that the Trial Advocate has proven that the murder of the decedent, Sergeant Arnold Quinn, was willfully and with forethought committed by the defendant, Lieutenant Charles Winston—while he, the defendant, was of sound mind and in full possession of all his faculties."

Colonel Thompson rapped with his gavel and said, "So be

it! This court is adjourned until nine-thirty tomorrow morning, at which time those having business before it will appear here again!"

Moscow gathered his papers together, rising with Adams as the court rose. "Do you want to talk with Winston now?" Moscow asked.

"I don't want to talk to anyone now."

"You know that Harvey and I are having dinner with you, sir. I hope you feel better then."

"At the Palace?"

"Yes."

"I know you're in no mood to hear anything of the sort now, sir—but you're a damn good lawyer. I have to say that to you. I just wish Harvey could have seen it."

"Thank you, Lieutenant."

Outside, in the main entranceway, Major Kensington was waiting for Adams. "I'm really sorry, old chap," he said. "I had put myself up to it and stiffened my back while I was waiting around today. Now I'm ordered to return to my station immediately and prohibited from testifying."

"Yes," Adams said, and nodded.

"You don't seem surprised?"

"No, I'm not surprised, Major, not at all."

"I suppose you could get some kind of legal paper or something or a subpoena—you know what I mean—and force it? I'd just as soon you did."

"No, I can't. We're two separate armies."

"You mean because in this hole we're top dog?"

"That's what I mean."

"Well—it has been a pleasure to know you. I do hope you're not hurt too badly, Adams."

"Thank you, Major. I'll get along." Adams smiled.

170

☆ Monday 7.20 P.M.

Lieutenant Harvey Bender was understandably in excellent spirits. He had produced a handwriting expert in the last place in the world where you would expect to find one. He had carried out his orders, and since he was very young, he had begun to build Barney Adams into a hero of sorts. He told Adams and Moscow how he had gone to the university and then to the police, and finally to the newspaper—from whence they sent him back to the university with a letter of introduction to Professor Nahrawal Chatterjee. Professor Chatterjee, a small, withered and unassuming man, as Bender described him, was a Doctor of Philology, educated at Oxford, who had written a manual of comparative chirography —stressing the differences between the Eastern and Western script development.

"Now, by God," he said, "I deserve a small good conduct badge for that, don't I, Captain?"

"I suppose you do. Will he testify?"

"He will. No money either. He's a peculiar little duck. And by the way," he added, "Lieutenant Sorenson gave me this letter for you." He handed an envelope to Adams, who glanced at it and then put it in his pocket.

Whatever it was, Adams did not want to read it in front

171

of them. He wanted only to finish with this dinner and meeting and then go to sleep.

"I also heard about Burton." Bender nodded eagerly. "I wish I could have seen the job you did on him, Captain."

Moscow fixed him with a cold stare, and Bender became quiet without knowing what he had done.

"Suppose we finish eating and get down to work," Adams said. "If I don't act more joyous, it has nothing to do with you, Lieutenant Bender."

"I mean, if I said something wrong—"

"Oh, go ahead and eat," Moscow told him.

Hurt and bewildered, Bender returned to his food and began to eat silently and efficiently.

☆ *Monday 9.40 P.M.*

Alone in his room now, Barney Adams opened the letter from Kate Sorenson. "Dear Barney," it began.

I am writing what I would be unable to say to you directly. That is because I have never been too good with words. To begin with, I was notified of my transfer today. I put in for one five months ago. I suppose they decided to process it very quickly, because I'm booked on Air Transport to Egypt tomorrow on the two o'clock

172

flight. From Cairo, I go on to England, where I'll join a base hospital.

This above does not change what decision I had come to. It only makes it easier for me. I hope it will also make it easier for you.

If I was only a little younger and a little different, the night we spent together would be something I would want to treasure all my life. The way it is, I don't know. Any more than I really know why you are doing what you are doing.

I wish that I could separate myself and yourself from the Winston case, but I can't. Even if you believe in the kind of love you said you feel for me, you can't separate such a thing happening from the circumstances in which it happens. Can you? I would like to believe that love can happen the way you said it did happen. I don't believe it. Love must be a continuation of yourself—but such continuation cannot happen in terms of both of us together. The continuation would be too different, because whether you believe in such things or not, we do come from two separate worlds—each of them far apart from the other.

Maybe that's why I wouldn't let myself fall in love with you, as much as I might want to. And love is something you can control, I think. You must want to let it happen to you.

I read a book once where this happened to a man and a woman in wartime. The author made you believe it while you were reading, and then he didn't have any problems to solve because one of them died. Life is something else, isn't it?

We would have to understand each other and plan to

173

live with each other in real life, wouldn't we, Barney? But I don't think you would ever really understand me, and I know that I would never understand you. You are too many separate things. You have the beautiful little boy face that I had come to detest as a symbol of men who neither labored nor suffered but lived their lives on the gift of that face. You come from a wealthy background, where you knew only peace and love. You never had to think about where the next meal was coming from. I don't say all that is bad, but it is different. Too much different ever to straighten out to a point of understanding.

You are like a child. But you are also a man, and the man frightens me. You have innocence but you also have a terrible and terrifying sophistication. You control so well that everything important remains bottled up inside of you.

But above all, I kept asking myself—why, why are you doing this thing with the defense of Winston? Why is the life of this sick and evil man so important to you? I asked Max Kaufman to explain it to me, and he tried. But it was no good. My own case is nothing. If they're moving me, I am glad to be moved, and I haven't changed my decision to testify for you in the morning. But it won't be as easy for others as it is for me. That doesn't matter to you. It doesn't matter who will be hurt, who will be ruined, who will have his dreams smashed—so long as you win this case.

You see, as much as I try, I cannot get myself to believe that the main reason you want to win is something apart from your need to win. I wish I could believe that you were standing against the world for some high moral purpose that is central to your life, but I can't believe that.

I think I have been honest in trying to explain this thing to you, Barney. When I see you tomorrow, don't make it harder for either of us. That wouldn't help.

And it was signed, simply, "Kate Sorenson."

☆ *Tuesday 4.16 A. M.*

He awakened from dreaming about Gabowski again, and as he lay sweating and trembling under the mosquito netting, he said to himself: I really must talk to Kaufman about this dreaming. I can't go on waking up night after night with this dream. It's no way for a person to live.

Then he stretched out on his back and tried to compose himself to sleep, even though he knew quite well that there would be no more sleep on this night. He wanted to think about Kate Sorenson, but he couldn't. He felt no grief, no sense of rejection; insofar as he was able to comprehend his own feelings, he felt nothing at all.

He let his thoughts wander back through his life to a day when he was ten years old, and that was the day when he left for military school for the first time. At the door of their house he clung to his mother, his face pressed against her, his arms around her. He had thought to himself then: They'll

175

have to tear me away from her. They'll have to tear my arms off.

"Barney," his father said, very quietly.

"Let the boy have a minute more," his mother begged.

"Barney."

I'll never let go, never, he thought.

"Barney, the car is waiting."

Then he let go and turned his tear-stained face to his father, who said coolly, "Be a man now, Barney. That will be expected of you now at all times. You are the son of a soldier and the grandson of a soldier, and you are now going to learn to be a soldier yourself."

This was what he remembered now, lying in bed in that place so distant from where he was born and bred; and as the long hours before dawn passed, Barney Adams tried to piece together how and where he had failed his father or failed himself. But the flow of thought, as he well realized, was without importance or consequence. Nothing until now was of great consequence. And perhaps least of all, as he was coming to know, was the empty strut of being a hero.

☆ *Tuesday 9.40 A. M.*

Kate Sorenson was the first witness for the defense, and she began her testimony soon after the court convened. Baxter took her to the Judge Advocate Headquarters, and then he picked up Adams at the Makra Palace. Lieutenant Moscow was riding with him, and he took the opportunity to wonder whether Adams would not have another interview with Winston.

"Why, Lieutenant?"

"Well, sir—"

"Go ahead," Adams said.

"I mean—well, I don't want to talk out of turn. Harvey and myself, we're both in a peculiar position. We admire you a great deal and we feel that we have known you a long time, but when you come right down to it, sir—well, we don't know you enough to press our opinion."

"What is your opinion, Lieutenant? I'm asking for it."

"Let me put it this way. You're defending a man."

"Yes?"

"I mean, a man it is hard to defend. Still—well, you have to defend the man, sir. You can't just defend an idea."

"Do you think that I'm defending an idea, Lieutenant?"

"Well, to tell the truth—sometimes, yes, I do. A principle— let's say, a contention."

"No," Adams said thoughtfully. "That's not so. I'm defending Charles Winston. But I can't talk to him. You and Lieutenant Bender can talk to him if you wish. But I don't think it will make any significant difference."

Adams had tried to be truthful, yet he was not wholly truthful. He couldn't trust himself to talk to Winston, just as now, standing in front of Kate Sorenson in full sight of the court and all the others in the room, he could not trust himself to look at Charles Winston. Yet he knew what Winston was in the only way that he could state it in his own thoughts: Winston was a body, and inside the body, the soul was dying.

177

Winston sat silently, the eyes empty behind the metal-rimmed spectacles.

Kate Sorenson was composed as she gave her name and rank; asked whether she knew the defendant, Lieutenant Charles Winston, she nodded at him and said, "Yes. There he is."

"And when did you first see Lieutenant Winston, Lieutenant Sorenson?"

"The morning he was admitted to the NP Ward."

"What was his condition at the time, Lieutenant?"

"He was sick, in a state of shock and profound depression. His blood pressure was very high, his pulse rapid."

Major Smith objected, on the grounds that Lieutenant Sorenson was not competent to define his condition medically. Colonel Thompson upheld the objection and ordered question and answer stricken from the record. Colonel Thompson's face bore the marks of a sleepless night. His bloodshot eyes were angry and tired.

"May I ask her opinion, sir?"

"Not on a medical question, no—you may not."

"May it please the court, am I not allowed to ask Lieutenant Sorenson her opinion of the condition of another human being?"

Mayburt passed a note to Thompson, but he shook his head with annoyance and said, "No—no, you may not. Not under circumstances where it would be inevitably interpreted as a medical opinion. Lieutenant Sorenson is not a physician, and not competent to give medical evidence."

"Very well—Lieutenant Sorenson, what are your duties in your ward?"

"I am chief nurse."

178

"Then it was your duty, was it not, to assign Lieutenant Winston to a bed?"

"It was."

"Where did you assign him?"

"We have six psychopathic isolation rooms. Two of them were empty. I placed him in one of those rooms with a wardsman on inside attendance."

"Was this on Major Kaufman's instructions?"

"I know my work, sir. I was not instructed what to do in this case. It was routine accommodation."

"Who assigned the guard to Lieutenant Winston's room?"

"Major Kaufman did that. He called the Provost immediately, and a military police guard was in the ward within the hour."

"Now, Lieutenant, I am going to ask you what your own duties and responsibilities toward Lieutenant Winston were during the next five days. Try to answer my questions in terms of what you did, not in terms of Major Kaufman's instructions. Nor am I interested in any conversations between Major Kaufman and yourself. Now, what were your duties and responsibilities toward Lieutenant Winston?"

"Since he was a special case, he was put directly under my supervision—that is, in nursing terms."

"Did he have a private nurse at all times, Lieutenant?"

"I assigned a wardsman to be in the room at all times."

"Why did you take these measures?"

"Because he was a suicidal depressive."

Major Smith rose to object, but Mayburt said, "If you are going to offer an objection, Major, I would like to note that the witness is merely specifying details of her work."

"May it please the court, I still object."

179

With Mayburt's comment on the record, Thompson had no other course open than to overrule.

"How often did you see the patient, Lieutenant?"

"I took Lieutenant Winston's pulse and temperature three times each day. I saw him at least six times each day. I spoke with him. I supervised his physical therapy—that is, baths and massage."

"Did he make any attempt to communicate with you, Lieutenant?"

"You asked me not to repeat conversations. He spoke to me quite often, as I said. I seemed to have his confidence."

"Did he communicate anything in writing?"

"Yes, he wrote a letter to me, which he gave me on the fourth day after he was admitted."

Adams went to the table and took a sheet of paper which Moscow held out to him. He gave the paper to Sorenson.

"Will you examine that, Lieutenant, and tell me whether this is the letter Lieutenant Winston wrote to you."

"This is the letter," she said, handing it back to him.

Adams asked that it be stamped for identification and entered as evidence. Wells and Jacobs scribbled furiously and passed notes to Smith, who rose and asked whether he could see the letter.

He read it hastily and then said, "I object to this being put in evidence as a letter to Lieutenant Sorenson from Lieutenant Winston. There is no evidence that Lieutenant Winston wrote this. May it please the court, unless Lieutenant Winston testifies to the authenticity of this letter, there is no way of proving that he wrote it."

Thompson reached for the letter, read it, and then passed it to Mayburt. The letter went along the line of officers.

"What is your opinion on this point, Captain Adams?" asked Thompson.

"I have Lieutenant Sorenson's testimony."

"You must have anticipated this, Captain?" Mayburt said.

"Yes, sir, I did."

Suddenly speaking up, Major Cummings said, "I'm no lawyer, but I find it difficult to understand why that letter shouldn't be read into the record. Could you give us an opinion, Colonel Mayburt—in terms of the law?"

"I would prefer that the court heard Captain Adams first. How did you anticipate this, Captain Adams?"

"I have a handwriting expert who is prepared to testify."

"How is he qualified and who is he?" Mayburt asked curiously.

"His name is Professor Nahrawal Chatterjee, and he is Full Professor of Philology at the local university. He took his degree at Oxford, and his thesis for his doctorate was a study of comparative chirography, based on historical deviations from original scripts."

Colonel Burnside, speaking for the first time, said in his slow, pleasant drawl, "I am sure, Captain, that you can make it a little clearer for us uninitiated ones."

"Yes, sir—chirography is the science of handwriting. Dr. Chatterjee studied the manner in which script writing evolved in the West and in the Orient, and attempted to explain the variations. I have not had time to read his book, but only to glance through it. He has been called upon by the local constabulary on four separate occasions. He has also testified on occasion at the litigation of wills."

"I would say that he is sufficiently qualified—wouldn't you, sir?" Mayburt asked Thompson, who had no choice but to agree and order the witness to be brought into the court. He

181

told Lieutenant Sorenson to stand down, but not to leave the courtroom.

Professor Chatterjee came into the court, and studied it with curiosity and diffidence as he was sworn in. He was a thin, nearsighted man of about sixty, stooped, white-haired, and wrapped in the folds of white cotton that constituted the native dress of the land. He looked at the letter, read it carefully, and then examined the specimens of Winston's handwriting that Bender had obtained early that morning in the presence of a military police witness.

"Professor Chatterjee, are both documents written by the same person?"

"Oh, yes. Yes, indeed—without any question of doubt." His voice was thin and high-pitched, his accent the precise and singular result of Oxford. "You see, Captain, such handwriting as this cannot be imitated except perhaps by a professional forger. To a very large extent, it is uncontrolled and emotionally blocked. At one point the *t*'s are upright, at another they lie over, as do the *l*'s and *d*'s. Here and there—an unfinished word. The uneven enlargement and diminution of the letters demonstrate considerable emotionable instability."

"In your opinion, sir, is this the writing of a sane man or an insane man?"

Major Smith rose, but before he could speak, Thompson snapped out, "You will not answer that question!" And to Adams, "You know that he is not competent to answer that question. That is a question for a physician, not for sideshow fakery!"

"May it please the court," Adams said, "and with all due respect, I must object to the court's comment and ask that it be stricken from the record."

182

"I think you forget yourself, Captain Adams."

"I am trying not to forget myself, sir."

"May I ask you to explain that comment?"

"May it please the court, I am merely trying to act within the framework of proper procedure. With all due respect, I repeat my request."

"Your request is denied, sir!"

Meanwhile, Mayburt had passed a note to Thompson—a note which brought an angry shake of Thompson's head. A second note followed this.

Then, unexpectedly, Colonel Burnside interrupted once more with his pleasant drawl, "Would the court have any objections to my putting that same question to the witness?"

Taken aback, Thompson passed the question on to Mayburt, who said, "I see no reason why the witness should not testify within his own competency. There have been cases where tests and drawings have been used to measure emotional balance." And to Chatterjee, he said, "Are such matters procedural within the limitations of your science, professor?"

"To a degree. I have no desire to indulge in what one might call side-show proceedings. I cannot describe people or read character from handwriting. But emotional factors have been carefully and scientifically charted."

"Then I see no way in which the court can deny your question, Colonel Burnside," Mayburt said carefully.

Burnside repeated the question, and Chatterjee answered, "In my own opinion, sir, I must say that this is the handwriting of an insane man."

☆ Tuesday 10.37 A. M.

Lieutenant Winston raised his head and fixed his watery eyes on Kate Sorenson as she began to read the letter. It was the first time Adams had seen any evidence of hurt or sorrow upon his face. As she read on, the corner of Winston's mouth began to twitch slightly and his eyes became bright with tears.

Dear Kate,
I call you so because to me I know someone right away. I don't have to try. When I saw you this morning God cut my belly. I put my hand down there and there was some blood so God cut me maybe with a dagger. That was a signal. This is a woman for you Winston— God said. And I am going to change everything now. I was waiting for you. Not me—God said that. So I have chosen you to be next to me I will give you money and you can live like a queen. I am only pretending to remain in here. I will walk out when I want to. I will spit in the face of the lousy mp at the door. They are all laughing at me but I am laughing at them. You are lucky that I like you.

184

It was signed, "Winston."

She finished reading and looked at Adams, now for the first time with tenderness and hopelessness. Then she looked past him at Winston, who leaned his elbows on the table and covered his face with his hands.

"After Lieutenant Winston gave you the letter and you had read it, what did you do with it?"

"I showed it to Major Kaufman. He read it and then he gave it back to me."

"Did Lieutenant Winston make any further reference to the letter?"

"No—he made no reference to it ever again."

"Did you ask him to show you where the bleeding was—the bleeding referred to in the letter?"

"I asked the wardsman to look for it. But there was no wound, no bleeding."

"Thank you," Adams said. And to the court, "May it please the court, I have no other questions of this witness."

Major Smith's cross-examination was brief. He asked a series of questions as to the rationality of Winston's conversation and actions. Was he able to tell time? Read a newspaper? Discuss events? Remember things that had happened the day before? Adams raised no objections, and Sorenson answered practically all of the questions in the affirmative.

It was twenty minutes after eleven when Lieutenant Sorenson had finished her testimony for Smith. Adams waived any redirect examination, and Thompson instructed the witness to stand down.

Then Thompson said, "I am releasing this witness from any further responsibility to this court, since she is under travel orders for this afternoon. Does either counsel have reason to object to this—or further require her presence?"

185

Both Adams and Smith shook their heads.

Thompson said to Adams, "I understand, Captain, that you have only one more witness to examine?"

"That is correct, sir."

"Very well. In that case, we will recess immediately and reconvene a half-hour past noon. This court will now recess."

Adams went to his table, where Moscow was gathering the papers and repacking the briefcase. Adams said to Bender, "Get an empty room here where I can talk to Winston."

"The MP?"

"Let him be there—I don't care about that. And Lieutenant Moscow, suppose you see if you can find us a few sandwiches and some beer or something. We won't have time to go out to eat. Get enough for Winston, too. I think they have a mess of some sort in the basement here."

"I'll get the sandwiches, sir, don't worry."

Adams hurried from the room just as Kate Sorenson was leaving.

☆ *Tuesday 11.30 A. M.*

Adams had to push his way through the reporters and out-side before he found a place to have a moment alone with Kate Sorenson, and then, with a sense of utter despair, she said to him, "What good is it, Barney? We can't say anything that will make it any better."

186

"Will it make it worse, Kate?"

"Don't argue now."

"I am not going to argue," he said. "I am not going to try to change your mind at all. I just want to spend a moment with you and say good-by decently."

"We can't say good-by decently, Barney."

"Give me a chance."

"I'm trying to give myself a chance."

"All right, it will be the way you want it to be. Let Baxter take you back to the hospital or to the airport—or wherever you must go now. The jeep is right over there."

He took her arm and they walked toward the jeep. She began to cry quietly, as if this were a reaction apart from herself. She could not control it and said, "I didn't want to cry, you see."

Adams shook his head hopelessly. He helped her into the jeep, while Baxter watched both of them silently and curiously.

"Take Lieutenant Sorenson wherever she has to go. She'll have her valpack. Help her with it. Stay with her until the plane leaves, Corporal, and then come back here."

"O.K., Captain."

"I hope England is good for you," Adams said. "It's a nice place, cool and kind."

"Thank you, Barney," she whispered. "I don't want it to be dark all around you."

"It has been for a long time."

"It will change."

"I hope so," he said.

☆ Tuesday 12 Noon

"Why are you trying to prove that I'm crazy?" Winston demanded of him.

"I'm not trying to prove that. I am defending you on the grounds that you are sick. You are sick, you know."

"Don't defend me! What mother-friggen right you got to defend me? I don't want to be defended!"

"You have to be defended. Neither of us have any choice about that, Lieutenant Winston. Now, I want to ask you some questions, and I want you to answer them."

"Go to hell!"

"That doesn't get either of us anywhere."

The corner of Winston's mouth began to twitch again. He covered his face with both hands.

"I want to know as well as you can tell me exactly what happened between you and Quinn on the night you killed him—what happened before he left you?"

Winston's skinny body began to shake spasmodically. He kept his hands pressed to his face. A minute went by. Adams repeated his question.

"It's no use, Captain," Bender said. "Oscar and I tried to question him. It's no use."

188

Winston let his hands drop. His eyes were listless now, as if a film had been drawn across them.

"Try to eat something," Adams said.

He didn't respond. He was alone now.

There was a note of pity in Adams' voice as he asked Winston whether he would have a cigarette. It made both Bender and Moscow glance at him sharply. Adams lit the cigarette and handed it to Winston.

"It's all right, Lieutenant," Adams said, thinking: As right as it will ever be.

☆ *Tuesday 12.45 P.M.*

After Major Kaufman had been sworn in and had given details of rank and position, Adams asked him to describe the events of the morning in question.

There was an electric quality in the courtroom on this afternoon. Outside, the clouds were gathering for rain. The heat was heavy and oppressive, and the ceiling fans, moving so slowly, appeared to be turning in liquid. Major Kaufman sat erect and withdrawn, the object of the whole population of the room, the officers of the court watching him seriously and intently, Major Smith and his two assistants sitting with the impatient frustration of hunters. The observers also watched and waited. Even Winston was intermittently held by the quality and mood of the place.

The thought came to Adams that this was a sanctuary—the only sanctuary in a world torn and twisted with every conceivable violence and hurt. But history was full of sanctuaries that crumbled.

Major Kaufman spoke to the court, yet he spoke through them and past them. Before he took the stand, he had offered no word or greeting to Adams. Adams could only wonder what his thoughts were—but such wonder and doubt were not a new experience during the last few days. Adams had come to ponder a great deal on the problems of a great many people.

"Lieutenant Winston," Major Kaufman said, "was brought to the hospital by two military policemen. That was early in the morning. These two policemen had been instructed by Major Kensington to bring their prisoner to the psychiatric section of the hospital. When the prisoner had been brought into our receiving room, Lieutenant Sorenson called for me. I came immediately, and as soon as I saw the prisoner, Lieutenant Winston, I realized that he was in a state of acute depression and, to some degree, shock."

"Mr. President?" Major Clement said to Thompson.

Thompson nodded, and Clement asked Kaufman, "How were you able to see that immediately, Major?"

"There were unmistakable signs. Depression translates into a condition of indifference. But the indifference is profound and pathological. The drive to live, to exist, a very important part of man's emotional structure, is submerged. When you have seen acute depression, you recognize it. Also, his breathing was labored. He sweated excessively. His facial muscles were without tone. And he was only in part aware of his surroundings—and therefore able to respond to those surroundings in a most limited sense. You must understand, sir,

190

that I am attempting to describe a medical phenomenon in lay language."

"I realize that," Clement replied.

Colonel Winovich wanted to know exactly what Major Kaufman meant by depression. "I have heard that term for two days now, like someone might say cholera. I've been depressed. I imagine you have, Major. Why treat it like some hellish disease?"

"Because it can be more hellish than most diseases, sir, and because it is a disease. When a normal person is depressed, he is not experiencing what we call, in a medical sense, depression—and, happily, most people never have that experience. I'll try to explain this as simply as I can. Depression, pathologically, is a combination of fear and hostility turned inward against the organism which is experiencing this fear and hostility. In its extreme form, it is a condition of total repression, total frustration, and total hopelessness. That is why we speak of the very deep depression as being suicidal. Most suicides are the result of this type of pathological depression, although many different mental conditions can bring about depression."

"Is this a physical condition, Major?" Thompson asked him. "Like heart disease or kidney trouble?"

"It has its physical aspects. It affects the entire organism rather than any single organ, and it is accompanied by changes in blood pressure, pulse beat and so forth. But the profound physical changes, I imagine, are chemical and have to do with various ductless glands and probably with the basic adrenaline-histamine balance."

"You say you imagine? Are you guessing? Don't you know?"

"There is a great deal about all disease that we don't know, sir, a great deal about the body that baffles all physicians. We

191

grope and guess and attempt to learn. As for diseases of the mind, well, until a generation ago they were for the most part treated no better or more wisely than in the Middle Ages."

"Did you examine the patient, Major?" Adams asked now.

"I did."

"How often?"

"I examined him physically when he was admitted—that is, I took blood pressure, pulse—listened to heartbeat and breathing, tested reflexes, examined his eyes and ears—the whole procedure of a thorough physical examination. I ordered a cardiogram, since his pulse was rapid and his blood pressure dangerously high, and a blood test and urine analysis. This was repeated two days later. Each day, he had a superficial physical. In addition to this, I examined him verbally each day for five days."

"What do you mean by verbally, Major?"

"That is a method of conversation or interview by which we attempt to more fully diagnose the nature of a psychosis. Actually, I ask questions. The patient answers them. I attempt to lead the conversation and to elicit salient points of knowledge."

"Now, when the patient was admitted, he was sick, was he not?"

"I should not have admitted him if he was not sick."

"Was his sickness at the time of admittance mental or physical?"

"There is no separating the two, Captain. A man's mind is a part of his body—his brain and nervous system, these are parts of the body. Lieutenant Winston was a very sick man when we admitted him. He has recovered in some part from the fatigue and shock which he was suffering then, and I

192

managed to bring his blood pressure down somewhat, but he is still a very sick man."

Major Smith rose with this and objected that Major Kaufman had no right to a diagnosis of a man he had not examined for weeks.

Mayburt put the objection aside, telling Smith, "We will not get into a dispute over this use of competence. The witness is a physician, and physicians are entitled to their observations as part of diagnosis."

"What is the nature of Lieutenant Winston's disease?" Adams then asked.

"Lieutenant Winston is suffering from paranoia. Paranoia is a generic term for a group of mental diseases which fulfill the terms of a general description. Medically speaking, I would describe paranoia as an organized irrational system of mentation and response—which is characterized by projecting into external society causation by unreal factors. It is persecutory in its direction and usually accompanied by intermittent depression."

"Could you describe it in lay terms, making the description at least in part a direct diagnosis of the defendant?"

Winston's interest had at last been wholly caught, and he watched witness and counsel with intense, trembling concentration.

"I can try, sir. Our habit is not to think these things through in ordinary language, and perhaps that is a fault. Let me begin by saying that the paranoid personality is not uncommon; but we do not consider people who have this personality pattern to be psychotic. We differentiate and ascribe the psychotic factor to the mind which organizes an entire irrational system. I am trying to simplify, but it is not easy.

"In the case of the defendant, the paranoid roots go back

to childhood, and even in childhood the irrational system was in process of organization. In other words, Lieutenant Winston began to create in his mind a picture of society in general and human beings in particular that departed more and more from the reality, until at last he was utterly incapable of coming to grips with reality. At this point, he became the prisoner of his own system.

"Why this happened, I cannot say. There are factors in our society that do this to children, but, I would speculate, only to children who have an area of specific weakness. These children develop a fear of people, a fear which increases with growth and intensifies itself constantly. And since this fear is unreal, without any foundation in society, it can be handled and controlled only with unreal defenses. Thus we get the persecution complex, which is the common and vulgar explanation of the paranoiac. But the paranoiac is basically afraid, and his fear is a disease, a sickness which so far society has not been able to cure.

"The paranoiac, as he matures, has only two choices—either to cope with his fears or to destroy himself. When he sets out to cope with his fears, he begins to fulfill a pattern which has come to be known as the power compulsion. Again, a misleading vulgarization. It is not power in itself which the paranoic is driven to command—for power in itself is meaningless—it is power over those whom he fears. And since he fears all mankind, the accomplishment of power can never cure or even balance the paranoiac. It is only an analgesic, a temporary assuagement of his terrors.

"The other alternative is depression—and its ultimate conclusion, suicide. When the paranoiac's defenses of power and authority over others finally crumble beyond hope of repair or reconstruction, then the fear begins to submerge his personality. His personality begins to disintegrate, and this disintegration is progressive. In a manner of speaking, he retreats into himself, cuts his connections with the outer and real world, turns his fear and hatred upon himself—and destroys himself. Even if prevented from suicide, this disintegration will continue and the soul will die. It is usually during this stage that he becomes delusionary. Bereft of real power, he invents power and sometimes comes to believe that he is a tool of God, or more usually, he the master of God and God the tool. Thus, he frequently places God within him, as part of himself."

They were all listening intently, Winston's face staring and fixed, only the tic on his mouth breaking the immobility, the court leaning forward over the table—even Smith caught, attentive and silent.

It was not Adams but Colonel Mayburt who broke the silence after Kaufman had finished, asking, "Did this breakdown—the beginning of this disintegration you speak of—did this come as a result of the murder of Sergeant Quinn?"

It was to the point, the key to the point; and Kaufman considered it before he answered. Then he said, "No. It was the other way around. Lieutenant Winston was the only commissioned officer at Bachree. He had the power and the authority. But Sergeant Quinn broke down this authority. He undermined Lieutenant Winston. He laughed at him and mocked him, and the process of disintegration began. The murder of Sergeant Quinn was the last desperate effort of Lieutenant Winston to defend himself with the exercise of power. But already, at that point, he was insane. Yes, he was insane then and he is insane now," Kaufman finished coldly.

Winston rose, pointed a shaking finger at Kaufman, and

195

screamed, "You're a lousy, mother-friggen Jew bastard liar! I'm sane! Sane! Sane—do you hear me, sane!"

☆ *Tuesday 1.40 P.M.*

Major Kaufman had identified his report and had read two paragraphs from it on the social connotations of paranoia. During this, there was no one in the courtroom who could forbear to glance at Winston. But they looked at a shell. The withdrawal of Charles Winston's soul and personality was almost an apparent physical fact. Beaten down and back by the scathing anger of Thompson, who had finally found an outlet and direction for his frustration and annoyance, Winston collapsed upon himself. His eyes became empty, his face slack. He sat at the defense table, his left hand upon the table, his right hand probing and examining his left hand.

Outside, the rain had started, strong and steady. Adams had just asked Kaufman what the purpose of his report was.

"Its main purpose, of course, is as a medical record—that is, a part of diagnosis and treatment. No physician worthy of the name will treat a patient without making a record of the case. In a situation like ours, with hundreds of patients entering and leaving the hospital each week, the report is essential. It goes with the discharged patient when further treatment is indicated, or it remains in our records for reference. Its secondary purpose is to supply information and data to the hospital command."

"Your report, Major, runs to eleven typewritten pages. Surely a report of that length is unusual?"

"Yes, sir—unusual but not unprecedented. I knew about the events at Bachree. Lieutenant Winston was a most unusual patient. He interested me, and I developed his case at some length. I also felt an obligation to my commanding officer to make his own position more tenable by supplying him with full and accurate medical data."

"More tenable? Did you suspect that his position might be untenable?"

"I did."

Major Smith began to rise, but Wells held him back almost physically, whispering in his ear. Moscow noticed this and said softly to Bender, "They're wrong. Adams won't hang himself. But now they're going to give him rope."

"Will you explain that?" Adams said to Kaufman.

"I knew of the feeling against Winston, the hatred and the bitterness. I knew that there would be pressures upon Colonel Burton."

Thompson interrupted sharply, "You know, Captain Adams, that this whole line is most improper. The witness cannot testify to unfounded gossip. This court knows of no pressures. You will strike that out, Sergeant Debbs."

Adams just glanced at Mayburt, who made no response at all to this.

"As the court pleases," Adams said, and then to Kaufman, "In any case, Major Kaufman, you felt that the Winston case was of sufficient importance and interest for you to report it at length and in detail?"

"That is so, Captain."

197

"And when you had completed this report, you took it to your commanding officer, Colonel Burton. Is that so?"

"More accurately, it was sent to him through regular channels."

"And he read it, sir?"

"I presume that he did."

"Then, concerning the report, Major, did Colonel Burton send for you?"

"He did."

"And what took place at that meeting with him?"

"We discussed the report, which he found unsatisfactory. He—"

"Please, Major—we can't take testimony as to what Colonel Burton said. However, with the court's permission, I would like to read a few lines of Colonel Burton's testimony to Major Kaufman, and then ask him whether this is to the best of his own recollection?"

Thompson hesitated, and then whispered to Mayburt, who said, "Would you bring the testimony in question to the bench, Captain Adams?"

Moscow was already underlining the passages in his notes, which he had typed out the evening before. He handed this to Adams, who took it to the bench. Mayburt and Thompson examined it, and then Mayburt said a few words, softly. Thompson shrugged. Mayburt gave the paper back to Adams and told him to proceed.

"I read now from the record, Major," Adams said, and read as follows:

" 'Did Major Kaufman submit his report to you before or after he refused to discharge Lieutenant Winston?'

" 'I believe it was before.'

" 'Did you read the report?'

198

" 'I did.'

" 'Did you read all of it, Colonel?'

" 'I read most of it.'

" 'Yet you saw fit to reject it?'

" 'As I told you some days ago, Captain Adams, the report was not competent or scientific.' "

Adams paused, and then added, "I read these few lines merely to fill in Colonel Burton's reaction to your report, according to his own testimony. Now, Major, did Colonel Burton reject your report?"

"He did."

"Were you instructed to prepare another report?"

"Yes, I was."

"And did you agree?"

"No, I refused."

"Why did you refuse, sir?"

"I refused because my report was both accurate and reliable, insofar as any knowledge of my own could determine. If I had prepared a second report, I would have changed nothing. I've spent my entire adult life in training for my profession and in the practice of my profession. Colonel Burton, sir, is not a psychiatrist. I am."

"Would you tell the court exactly what your training and professional background consist of, Major Kaufman?"

"I'll be happy to. I was graduated with honors from Belle-vue Medical School and I interned at Bellevue Hospital in New York. I had three years of psychiatric training, a year at the Phipps Clinic, a year and three months at Johns Hopkins Hospital, and nine months at the Menninger Clinic in Topeka, Kansas. I took three years of night courses in psychoanalytical training at the Institute in New York, and during this period I was on the staff at Bellevue Hospital, Staff Assistant and then Associate Attending Psychiatrist—in which position I continued after setting up in private practice of psychiatry. Two years before I enlisted in the armed services, I became an assistant professor in psychiatry at New York University Medical College. There is my training and my professional background, sir! Do you wonder that I refused to alter and falsify a report at the behest of Colonel Burton?" Kaufman finished hotly.

Major Smith objected. "Colonel Burton testified under oath, may it please this court! I must object strenuously to this irresponsible accusation!"

Colonel Mayburt took this in his own hands, and before Thompson could make any comment, he replied to Smith: "An objection in court is a legal procedure, Major. There is nothing in this testimony that calls for the court's sustaining such an objection. If you are expressing your indignation at the charge laid against Colonel Burton, you have the right to recall Colonel Burton or to institute separate proceedings on a perjury count—if the court so agrees."

He turned to Adams then and said, "Meanwhile, Captain Adams, I would like to question the witness further on this point."

Adams nodded. Colonel Thompson scribbled a note to Mayburt, and Mayburt answered softly, "Of course, Colonel Thompson." And then said to Kaufman: "You understand, Major Kaufman, that you have made a most serious accusation. I also feel that you have spoken in some heat—and that possibly a connotation is placed upon your statement that is not entirely warranted. Yesterday, in his cross-examination of Colonel Burton, Captain Adams asked him whether he had advised you to change your conclusions. Colonel Burton answered, and I quote him, 'I advised him to restudy the

200

case.' Then Captain Adams asked Colonel Burton, I quote, 'Did you advise him—Major Kaufman—to find Lieutenant Winston sane?' Colonel Burton's answer was the same as for the previous question. Now I am asking you, sir, did Colonel Burton instruct you to prepare a report which would find the prisoner sane? In other words, did he spell this out?"

"No, sir, he did not," Kaufman replied.

"Did he instruct you to change your conclusions?"

"He suggested that I change my conclusions."

"He refused to accept your report?"

"That is right, he refused."

"Then you must realize that your charge of falsification is unsupported. I would suggest that you withdraw the remark and apologize to the court for its intemperance."

For a long moment Kaufman was grimly silent. Then he nodded. "I withdraw any suggestion of falsification and I apologize to the court."

"I think that is sufficient," Mayburt said. "You may continue to question the witness, Captain Adams."

"Thank you, sir," Adams agreed, drawing a long breath of relief. "Now Major, here is your report. Would you read from it the conclusions to which Colonel Burton objected."

He handed the report to Kaufman, who turned to the final page and read: "In the light of the above, certain diagnostic conclusions are unavoidable. Lieutenant Winston is a psychotic paranoiac in an advanced stage of acute depression and personality disintegration. Under present conditions, prognosis is entirely negative. Under conditions existing in the United States, he might be temporarily responsive to shock therapy, and the depression might be interrupted with recessive periods. In either case, it is my opinion that no recovery is possible.

"In a medical-legal sense, Lieutenant Charles Winston is insane, and cannot be held legally responsible for his actions during a period of at least three weeks before the murder of Sergeant Quinn, during the act of murder, or since that time.

"In a physical sense, he must be specified for hospital confinement; and under no circumstances could I discharge him except in transit to another hospital in the custody of the U.S. Medical Corps. He is a suicidal depressive who must be under observation at all times, and his personality disintegration is so rapid that total collapse may be expected in a matter of months."

Kaufman then handed the report back to Adams, who laid it on the court table and said to Kaufman, "Did Colonel Burton question your diagnosis and conclusions?"

"He did."

"Did he refuse to accept your statements on Lieutenant Winston's legal and medical sanity?"

"Yes, sir, he refused."

"Were you advised to rewrite the report?"

"Yes, I was so advised."

"Did he state that Lieutenant Winston was sane?"

Major Smith rose and offered his objection on the grounds of hearsay. The court ordered the last two questions and answers to be stricken from the record.

"Let me rephrase that question," Adams said. "Did you refuse to rewrite the report, Major?"

"I did."

"And did Colonel Burton order you to discharge the defendant, Lieutenant Winston?"

Again Major Smith rose, but Mayburt shook his head and said pointedly, "This will be allowed, sir. We are not a

202

civilian court. We are a court of the United States Army, and we must allow a certain flexibility on questions of discipline and authority."

"He did," Major Kauman answered.

"And did you refuse to obey that order?"

"I told Colonel Burton that he could not order me to discharge a patient who was seriously sick; that if I complied with such an order, I would be criminally negligent and that it would violate every ethic I held as a physician."

At this point Colonel Burnside leaned forward and said, "I'd like to ask the witness a question, Mr. President—by your leave, of course."

Thompson's agreement was defensive, as it always was when confronted by a Regular Army man on the bench.

Burnside asked, his voice lazy and curious at once, "Tell me now, Major Kaufman, just what are your own feelings toward the defendant?"

"I hate his guts," Kaufman answered, spacing each word and underlining it with deliberate emphasis.

"Now that's a strange answer for a psychiatrist, isn't it, Major?"

"Why, sir? Should I have charity, sympathy, love for a man who embodies all that is vile, outrageous and hateful to me?"

"Yet, by your own testimony, sir, he is sick."

"Yes—physically sick. And as a physician I will give whatever strength and skill I have to cure his sickness. There is where my duty lies. I don't have to love him."

"Then tell me, sir, why did you put yourself in the position you did and refuse to carry out the orders of your commanding officer?"

203

"Because a physician has an obligation prior to his own emotions or needs."

"Obligation—to whom, sir?"

"To his practice of medicine."

☆ *Tuesday 2.45 P.M.*

"I have no further questions," Barney Adams said, and then told Major Smith, "You may cross-examine, sir."

Major Smith looked at him bleakly, rose, and said, "May it please the court—I have no questions."

"And I have no other witnesses, Mr. President," Adams said. "The defense rests its case."

Colonel Thompson said, "You may have a few minutes to prepare your closing remarks, Captain Adams."

Adams thanked the court and walked back to his table. The lights were on in the room, yet he felt a brooding and oppressive darkness. He felt tired and used up, and could not for the life of him anticipate what he would now say.

He confided this to Moscow as he sat down.

"Whatever you say, it will be all right," Moscow replied.

☆ Tuesday 2.55 P.M.

It was just a few minutes before three o'clock when Barney Adams rose to make his closing remarks. It seemed to him then that while, in one sense, the case was finished, in another sense it was only beginning. It had happened too quickly. When he turned and met General Kempton's eyes and saw the thin trace of a smile on the general's face, he had the strange feeling that they had not yet met and not yet confronted each other.

He would be confronting him now, he realized.

He addressed the court and said, "May it please the court— I will try to make my summation as brief as possible, yet there are a number of things I feel that I must touch upon. I trust that the court will forgive my mentioning that this is the first case I have ever participated in as a trial counsel. For that reason, I have blundered here and there, and I have done poorly what could have been done well. I offer this as no excuse but only as an explanation. I was well trained for the courts of the United States Army. I have no excuses.

"When I began to examine the case of Lieutenant Charles Winston, I was appalled at the thought of conducting any sincere defense—"

He had to look at Winston now, but not at a man. The

205

skinny, bent figure was motionless, eyes fixed upon the table that supported him.

"—for there was no possible doubt as to who had committed the crime and how it was committed.

"The crime was witnessed by men whose word could not be challenged. So far as I knew, there was no sufficient provocation, and the manner of the crime was brutal and shocking. Yet even in the very first description of the crime that I read, there was for me an implication of something unnatural, awful and insane. It was this suggestion of insanity that drew me along a certain path of investigation—until I decided to make it my only defense. I decided to prove that Lieutenant Winston was insane, and this I have attempted."

Adams shook his head, rubbed his eyes and drew a deep breath.

"It hasn't been a pleasant experience," he said, "and I would not want to go through these seven days again. My war experience until now has consisted of infantry operations in Africa and in Italy, but I don't think that any part of it affected me so profoundly as this attempt to defend Lieutenant Winston. For, like Major Kaufman, I hate the man I am defending. I have not said this to anyone until now. I did not want to say it—ever; yet here and now I know that I must say it. Otherwise, all else that I have said is meaningless and fraudulent.

"I am being personal because this has been my connection with this case. I have lived through it personally and deeply. Time after time during this past week, I realized that Lieutenant Winston was the spiritual brother of what my country fights—in a life and death struggle. For, in Lieutenant Winston, there is that same composite that led the world to hell—ignorance, arrogance, hatred of all that is human, fear of all

206

that is human, racism, a lust for power and a whimper of persecution."

Adams stopped for a moment, swallowed, and took hold of himself. His voice had been rising. He controlled it now. When he continued, his voice was even, his tone muted.

"This was the man I had to defend. I have no doubt that he is insane. I have presented in this courtroom a witness I believe eminently qualified to pass judgment on such questions. I believe I have proven to the officers of this court-martial that Lieutenant Winston was and is insane and not responsible for his own actions. My experience with Lieutenant Winston, my conversation with him and with those who lived and worked with him, proved it to my own satisfaction. But there was something else that I could not explain or prove so easily—

"That is, why I felt the compelling necessity to prevent the execution of a man so depraved, so lost, and so apparently worthless. I felt this need. I had to understand why I felt it. I had to understand why, when the whole world has been turned into a charnal house, when the best and finest of our young men are being destroyed by the senseless, brutal savagery of a Hitler and a Hirohito—why, in these circumstances, a court must be convened and many hours of your time consumed in deciding whether or not a brutal murderer should be hanged. To a casual observer, it would make no sense—no, not simply to a casual observer, but to me it made no sense at first. None. It was a game we would play, without content or meaning.

"Well, I am trying to say this—and it isn't easy for me to say. I have been forced to try to understand a thing I know little of—very little indeed. But if the court will permit me and bear with me, I will tell it as best I may.

"It began for me when I had my first interview with Major Kaufman. We had talked about paranoia, about the difference between a neurosis and a psychosis, about the meaning and implications of insanity when approached from a social and medical point of view. Then the major was called away for an hour to make his rounds in the hospital. I asked him whether he could give me something to read on the subject of paranoia while he was gone. He gave me some case histories he had and he also gave me a copy of Plutarch's *Lives*. He suggested that I read the chapter on Alexander the Great, as a brilliant literary description of a paranoiac who influenced history.

"I had read this in school; now I reread it with horror and amazement. It was not what I had read before. It was the case-history of a madman who, in his lust for power and his fear of man, had blazed a path of death and destruction across half the world. Plutarch knew nothing of mental disease, but his careful and meticulous description of the actions of this conqueror had survived with meaning and validity. All of the elements to which Major Kaufman gave testimony were present, the fear and mistrust of his closest friends, the insatiable drive for conquest and power, the depressions, the obscene whimpering with which this always ends—all of it was there.

"I had to ask myself whether or not this was a poor comparison. It is hard for us to see Lieutenant Winston as an Alexander. It is less difficult to pass from him to Adolf Hitler. And it is utterly frightening even to suspect that millions of good, decent and innocent human beings must die because a Winston holds a club of ultimate power.

"I am making no diagnosis of these men in the seats of the mighty. I know very little about mental illness—only the fragments that I have picked up in the course of this case.

But I have come to understand one thing—that this court convened here now, in the midst of the greatest war mankind ever knew, is not a piece of mummery or manners. Quite to the contrary, may it please you, the officers of this court—quite to the contrary, a part of the essence of this struggle resides here in this court.

"For here in this court, and this I know, Lieutenant Charles Winston will be judged apart from my hatred of him, apart from the contempt and the disgust that people may feel for him. He will be judged by a system of law that men have fought and died to achieve—and because here, here in this court of the United States Army, we go through this procedure, we prove ourselves, our struggle and the values we ask men to die for.

"We have won and organized a system of law which says, in effect, that when a man's mind is mortally sick, he cannot be held responsible for his actions nor punished for those actions.

"I know of nothing more important than this seemingly ritualistic concern for the rights of a single individual—I know of nothing better that man has built, nothing more precious, nothing more holy to defend—to die for if need be. And it seems to me that not the least important action in this long and desperate struggle that involves all of us—will be the demonstration to the whole world that ours is a system of law. No man is above this law, none below it, and if we spoil it or breach it or corrupt it in one place, no matter what the necessity, we do ourselves irreparable hurt.

"Under this law, Lieutenant Charles Winston must be found not guilty—for, I believe, we have heard sufficient evidence to the effect that he is insane and thereby not to be held responsible for his actions. May it please the court and the officers of this court, I submit this plea and ask that a verdict of not guilty be given."

As he finished and walked back to his place, Barney Adams realized that his summation had been inadequate, brief in length even for a military court, touching on none of the finer points of evidence, and adding nothing to Major Kaufman's remarks. His only achievement, as he saw it, lay in the fact that he had said something—whereas when he began, there was nothing he knew that he could say which would make any appreciable difference.

He sat down in silence between Bender and Moscow, but they said nothing to him. He was afraid to face their eyes, nor was he aware of the silence and tension in the whole of the courtroom.

He hardly listened now as Major Smith spoke. Major Smith mocked at what he termed "groping sentimentalities" and at the resurrection of Plutarch as a witness; he went into the evidence, challenged Major Kaufman, defended Colonel Burton and pleaded with the court not to allow the world to laugh and sneer at American justice.

"I have heard many fine words here today," he concluded, "and a good many half-baked theories. The fact remains that the defendant committed a brutal, an unspeakable murder— yes, by the testimony of his own counsel. He was sane enough to command the post at Bachree before he did this act of murder. He was sane enough to murder a man. And he is sane enough to know that insanity is his only defense. May it please the court—this man, Lieutenant Charles Winston, was not too insane to kill. We submit that he is sane enough to pay the price for his crime, that he must pay this price, so that the men of our armed services and the people of the whole world may know that murder does not go unpunished under American law.

"Therefore, I ask that the defendant be found guilty as charged—guilty of murder in the first degree."

When Major Smith finished his peroration and resumed his seat, Colonel Thompson talked to Mayburt in whispers—for perhaps two minutes. Then he called for attention with his gavel and said, "The court will now recess while the officers of the court-martial attempt to come to a verdict. The Provost is informed that the prisoner is to remain on the premises until otherwise instructed. Counsel for the defense and for the prosecution will also remain on the premises of the Judge Advocate General.

"Court is now recessed."

☆ *Tuesday 4.20 P.M.*

Adams found Moscow and Bender on either side of him, fending off the press, Bender telling them, "Look, have a heart. Captain Adams hasn't had a moment to rest or relax for three days now. You know he isn't permitted to comment."

"No comment then," one of them agreed. "Just a statement —anything, Captain. How do you feel about it? Are you glad it's over?"

"He can't comment—on anything—you know that!" Bender snapped. The two lieutenants moved along on either side of him, clearing a way and fending off questions. Corporal Baxter had come into the broad foyer of the building, and he joined them and added his bulk to the little group around Adams.

Bender led them into the corridor opposite the courtroom, opened a door, and told Adams, once they were inside the small room, "This is our room for the rest of today, sir. You can relax and just take it easy here."

"I wanted to talk to Major Kaufman," Adams protested.

"No, sir," Baxter said. "He went straight back to the hospital. I took him there."

Adams nodded and dropped into a chair. "Funny I'm so damned tired," he said. "I feel it in the back, where I was cut up. God, I'm tired."

"Anything I can do, just ask me, Lieutenant," Baxter told Bender.

"Sure," Bender replied. "Look, Corporal, we're going to be here for a good long spell, and I suppose the Judge Advocate will break their hearts and feed us, but God knows when that will be! Can you pick up some cold beer and a couple of tins of those limey crackers they call biscuits—the salty kind, not the sweet stuff." He stuffed a handful of bills into Baxter's palm. "Make sure the beer is cold, and if it's in tin, get an opener. O.K.?"

"Sure, Lieutenant. Do you want cigarettes, too?"

"Might as well. We're bound to run out."

The corporal was at the door when Adams said, "Baxter?"

"Yes, sir."

"Did you see her onto the plane?"

"Yes, sir. I helped her with her valpack."

212

"Was she all right?"

"She was all right, Captain."

"What kind of a plane was it—not one of those damn C46's?"

"No, sir—it was a C47—a real nice plane, no bucket job, but seats and upholstery and the whole works."

"Thank you, Baxter."

"What the hell, Captain, it was nothing," he said, and then he went out.

Adams lit a cigarette and sat in silence, smoking. For a little while neither Bender nor Moscow said anything. Their silence irritated Adams. He had never felt just like this before, tense and tired and nervous as a cat, and finally he burst out at them, "Damn it to hell, say it!"

Bender looked at him curiously. Moscow asked softly, "Say what, sir? I wanted to say something. There are times when you don't know what to say."

"You're both lawyers. Tell me how I loused it up! There's no need for courtesy. It's done with. A week from now I'll be on my way out of here."

"You didn't louse it up," Moscow whispered. "So help me God, I think you won the case."

"How—by doing everything wrong, even that Boy Scout closing? By parading my stinking little bit of knowledge? By destroying Burton, a setup if ever there was one, and ten times the man that rat Winston ever was? How?"

"That Boy Scout closing," Bender said, "was the most moving thing I ever heard in a courtroom. I didn't say anything. What could I say, sir?"

"You didn't try the case right," Moscow said. "It broke my heart the way you fought and struggled your way through

213

it. But I think if you had tried the case any other way, you wouldn't have had the chance of a snowball in hell."

"I was rotting here," Bender said. "I was hating myself and the whole world, stuck in this lousy, festering ass-hole of the universe. And I'll continue to rot here because that miserable bastard Thompson can't stand for me to keep my nose pink. But I won't hate myself any more. Not after today."

"What did you expect us to say?" Moscow demanded. "What in hell do you say to someone like yourself, sir? You tell me."

"You came here Wednesday—Wednesday," Bender said, "one lousy week ago."

Choking with something he had never felt before, hardly able to get the words out, Adams stood up and said, "Damn you—get out of here, both of you! Leave me alone for a while! You can't be alone ten minutes in this mother-friggen army!"

☆ *Tuesday 6.25 P.M.*

They were sitting in the little room, finishing the last of the beer and listening to Baxter's story of how two girls held up the filling station in Nashville one night, when Sergeant Candyman knocked at the door and then entered with a tray of sandwiches and a pot of coffee.

214

"They should have just let us starve," Baxter said.

"The hell you're starving!"

"What is your status, Candyman?" Bender demanded. "Are you a spy or a God damned Saint Bernard dog?"

"I'm just a neutral, sir," Candyman said. "They needed help. There's a lot of feeding around here tonight."

"Leave him alone," Adams said.

"Candyman—what do we drink the coffee out of, the pot?" Bender demanded.

"I'll ask the general, sir."

"You do that," Bender agreed.

Candyman put down the sandwiches and coffee, smiled at them, and left. Only Bender began to eat. Adams said to Moscow, "Want some air, Lieutenant?"

They went outside to the garden. The rain had stopped, and the air was sweet and clean and fragrant in the twilight. The sighing wind brought its medley of odor, the jasmine, the scent of roses in the garden, the sharp tang of charcoal and dung burning. In the sky a lacework of clouds glowed in every shade of orange and purple, and against this color a single great vulture wheeled and swooped.

"I suppose one could become used to this," Adams reflected.

"One could."

"I suppose, in time, you could come to love it."

"I think I love it, sometimes," Moscow confessed. "I'm beginning to understand it, a little."

"It takes time," Adams said, his first regret like a sharp twinge inside of him. "I'll be going away—and I won't want to go."

"No, you don't want to go away. That's the strangest part of it," Moscow said.

215

☆ *Tuesday 9.40 P.M.*

By half-past eight all conversation had stopped. Baxter had taken the jeep to the car pool for gas. Adams, Moscow and Bender had spent the last hour in silence. They were still silent when there was a knock at the door. Moscow opened it.

A military policeman there said, "The court is convening now, sir. Will you take your places?"

They walked through the hall in the same silence. Kempton was still there, as were his guests, but they walked apart from Adams and his group, nor did the general even glance at him.

At the doors to the courtroom, Adams and the two lieutenants waited for Winston to pass them. Two MP's were with him. One of them ventured to support his arm; he shook himself free. He walked into the courtroom and sat down. The others followed him. They remained standing.

Thompson was pale, his eyes bloodshot. When he told them to be seated, his voice shook just a little.

Adams studied the officers of the court-martial, but there was nothing to be read from their appearance. They were tired, and their faces were set and expressionless. Their eyes sought no one and conveyed nothing.

"I don't care now," Adams told himself. But that was not

true; he had cared more and about more things this past week than ever before in his life. He had cared more deeply and felt more poignantly than ever before—and he still cared. He had struggled with thoughts that were new, with words that were unfamiliar, and with concepts unclear and only half formed.

He had a sense of failure, of inadequacy and defeat. But he still cared; that had not changed.

"Will the prisoner stand," Colonel Thompson said.

Winston rose to his feet. He did not look at Thompson or at Adams, but only at his hands, which he held trembling at his waist.

"The court has come to a verdict," Thompson continued. "The court finds that the prisoner is not guilty and orders that he be returned to the General Hospital for further treatment."

Winston gave no evidence of having heard anything at all. He stood as he had been. Adams heard himself saying, in a hoarse whisper, "I'm glad it's done."

*　*　*　*　*

Adams had taken his company back from the front to the rest area at Okinawa, and their mail was waiting. Among his letters was one from Major Kaufman, the first communication since they had parted some five months before. He read it eagerly.

I hope this finds you in good health. I have no idea where you actually are now, but I think I might guess. Will it surprise you to hear that in so short a time the Winston affair is practically forgotten? Not only did it fail to split the Grand Alliance, but strangely enough the decision ended some of the ill feeling in this theater.

Winston, poor devil, managed to cut his wrists on the way back to stateside and he was buried at sea. I can feel a twinge of pity for him now. From Sorenson, I had a note only a few days ago—the first in a long time. She just married a British merchant seaman, the first officer on an armed cargo ship. Not many details. She speaks of him as a decent fellow, and she may remain in England when this long and weary war ends.

I know that you became fond of Oscar Moscow, one of your assistants at the trial—and it's a bitter thing to have to tell you about his death. He volunteered for service in Burma—I guess you read about that operation —and his request was granted all too eagerly. He was killed in action there—I don't suppose he had it in him to be much of an infantryman. Harvey Bender was very close to him and very deeply affected by his death. He holds Thompson responsible, but I think he's all wrong there. Moscow did what he had to do, and only he was responsible.

For myself, my prediction was remarkably accurate. I am dispensing drugs, counting atabrine pills, and tending to all the various and sundry ailments that flow into our dispensary at the end of the narrow gauge, about seventy miles past Bachree and in the same stinking jungle. My only solace is the day or two each week that I spend with Major Kensington—you remember him, of course. We play cribbage, a foolish game he taught me.

One more note on my own fate—and I imagine this will interest you. Before I left, General Kempton called me in to Headquarters. I had a brief hope that he intended to recognize my small talents and employ them, but he immediately made it plain that he had no intentions of

218

interfering with Colonel Burton's decisions. He pointed out that as Theater Commander he stood apart from such things. Then he sat me down, gave me a cigarette, became as charming as the occasion demanded, and wanted to know whether it was my idea to testify—that is, my very own.

Of course, he pointed out that I was not obligated to tell him, but I saw no reason not to. I said that you had persuaded me—that left to my own devices, I'd have had neither the guts nor the desire to stick my neck out.

"And you did this because Barney Adams talked you into it?" he said.

I said that you had not talked me into anything except a sharp and clear look at myself—and then I had recognized the simple necessity of living with myself.

He didn't buy this easily, but the truth is that you were his problem, not me. He said this and that and then came to the heart of the matter—what devil drove Barney Adams?

Why ask me, I wanted to know—and he said words to the effect of my being a psychiatrist and therefore under some obligation to understand why men did the things they do. Well, I replied that the approach was fallacious. You were not sick, and therefore no more my problem than his. But I offered a guess—a poor one, I suppose. I said that a thoughtful soldier can suffer a particular agony of his own, and that it becomes almost an implacable necessity to balance killing with some rational purpose.

I don't know whether he saw what I meant, although your Kempton is far from a fool. He replied that whatever his own feelings were concerning one Barney

Adams, he refused to believe that you would not defend your country—whether or not you believed in your country's cause.

I had no quarrel with that. I only wondered—aloud—whether under such circumstances you could also defend Barney Adams.

"Then he was defending himself?" Kempton demanded.

"Or whatever he believed in," I replied, and pointed out that there were people to whom belief was of prime importance. He then wanted me to spell out this belief—re Winston, but I had no right to talk for you, and I left him perhaps no less troubled and bemused than I had found him.

For myself, I have thought about it more than I should, and I think I begin to comprehend the Winston affair. It does not bear easy explaining. It is almost a frightening thing to come to believe that no infraction of the laws that man made to defend man can be lightly tolerated, that the whole fabric is one, and that, ripped anywhere, it can threaten the whole. Is it this long and terrible war that has given some of us the feeling that the rights of man are holy beyond dispute? Or is that the single ray of light in the darkness that covers the world? I must confess that I don't know. The Winston case is something I feel very deeply, as I am sure you do, but I find it very hard to talk about.

So there is a very brief summary or postscript to the Winston affair. I should enjoy hearing from you sometime—if you find yourself with time on your hands. As with so many people one meets in a war, you want to know them better and longer. But the whole thing is too large and too much in motion.

My best—and all the good luck in the world.

He finished reading. A sergeant, passing by, asked him, "Good news, I hope, Captain?"

"Good and bad," Adams answered with a shrug.

He sat looking at the letter, a pang of incredible loneliness clutching his heart. It would always be there, he realized; it would never go away; the loneliness would temper and dull as time passed, but it would not go away.